695
6⁻

adventures with

JULIA

a novel by

CANDACE DENNING

north point press

SAN FRANCISCO · 1986

I want to thank especially Geoffrey Wolff.

For Daniel B.

adventures with
JULIA

JULIA *goes to a wedding*

Julia Murphy knew that the bride ironed her hair. She wondered how she ironed it close to the scalp and saw herself bent over, one ear to the ironing board, listening for its internal moan. The bride, her head bowed and her straight blond hair obscuring her face, could have been any bride.

The couple turned, Julia's cue to start playing "Wedding March." The bride looked bright but the groom was pallid. Julia wanted to cry. At other people's weddings she felt truly married to Michael. Afterward, walking up the aisle with him, she carried her music against her like schoolbooks and kept her eyes straight ahead on the windows at the back of the chapel where light entered in dusty shafts.

"How did you say they met?" Julia asked. She knew how they met. She and Michael were drinking champagne next to the Brie with almonds. The cheese was running all over the cut-glass platter. Julia eyed the bride across the candlelit reception hall. She was too old for white.

"I can't believe people who meet like that get married." Julia sighed. "Or that people getting married for the second time have big weddings. Or that ministers talk about modest, silent wives."

Michael moved his hand with the knife toward the pâté. The band was playing "Moonlight in Vermont."

"You're probably wishing for a well-trained wife, aren't you?" she said. She ate a white grape. "What's wrong?"

"Nothing," he said. He said it again. His face was paler than usual. Once, with his hair slicked back so his ears stuck out, Julia caught a glimpse of him as a twelve year old. Now she thought the next thing he was going to say would be a lie.

"Let's get out of here," he said. "Let's go over to McGraw's. There's something I have to tell you."

She liked the contrast they made walking in dressed up. McGraw's had formica tables and a warped linoleum floor. They sat in a wooden booth in a corner. A stocky waitress named Irene gave them menus and they ordered a pitcher of beer. Julia listened to the clack of billiard balls from the other side of the wall. Michael lit a cigarette. They watched the smoke float between them.

"Remember the blond in the red dress at the gift table?" said Michael.

"The bleached blond in the flame-red dress?"

"Her name is Anna," he said. "Anna and I were married for six months when I lived in Chicago." It sounded like a complaint.

Julia waited until she felt on her face the composed look of her mother.

"I'm relieved it isn't anything more recent," she said. They had been married seven years.

Michael laughed. "It was a mistake to begin with," he said, waving it aside. "The invitations were out, my best friends were coming, her family had reservations they couldn't cancel."

"She looks a lot older than you," Julia said. This reassured her. She touched his hand across the table, but he only stared at the pitcher of beer Irene had just set down.

"I knew she would come out for the wedding and I should have told you in advance. I'm sorry," Michael said.

It occurred to Julia to be angry, but she did not want to appear small-minded.

"Have you seen her?" she asked.

"We had lunch on Thursday."

"Did you sleep with her for old times' sake?" Julia tried to laugh but her lips trembled. She took a sip of beer.

"It isn't like that," he said.

Michael looked toward the bar and frowned. Julia stared at him as she would a stranger.

"I don't think about it anymore," he said. "It isn't important." He was watching the television above the bar.

Julia wanted to talk some more about it. She had a hundred questions but she said nothing. She was thinking of the day she saw Michael through the window of a bookstore. He had a book clasped against his crotch the way ministers held Bibles, and he was talking to someone hidden by a book display. Julia stopped to watch him through the heavy plate-glass window. In the parking space behind her, a car engine raced. Then Michael raised his face and laughed without sound. He was a nice-looking man laughing with his mouth wide open in a bookstore at noon. He was a man she didn't know.

Michael didn't laugh that way with her. When they were together, time became an irritating factor between them. Julia envied the other, invisible person. She wanted to pluck Michael from the moment.

Now, Michael put his hand over hers and they locked fingers. They sat holding hands across the wooden table and finished the pitcher of beer. They watched the end of the football game on television.

JULIA *has her future told*

Julia, dressed in black, walked with her chin high, not watching the buckled edges of cement. She did not trip once. Along the street grew trees with furry pink flowers.

"For twenty *thousand* dollars, who was the author of . . ." The voice was nasty. "Take your time," it said over a smear of organ music coming from one of the townhouses. A dog barked at Julia from behind a baby gate. She did not know why she had stopped her car to get out and walk in this neighborhood. Sometimes she felt that a strange woman inhabited her.

On the front of a gray house hung a small hand-painted sign. MADAME NORA, PALMIST AND SPIRITUALIST. TUESDAY SPECIAL — $2. Julia stopped. It was Tuesday.

She could have described the room without ever having seen it, the place looked so familiar. Just inside the door was a television of blond wood, turned up loud. A beige recliner sat tilted back in front of the television, and a mauve couch and a coffee table with potted violets on a crocheted mat were across the room. The house smelled of bacon, and somewhere there would be a Bible.

"May I help you?" The woman turned down the television. She was plump and had a full, congenial bosom.

"What is the two-dollar special?" said Julia.

"You ask me one question and I answer it," the woman said with a slight accent. She clasped her hands over her stomach. "For five dollars I give you a full reading."

"What is a full reading?"

The woman sighed.

"I'll have the full reading," Julia said, giving the woman five dollars.

As they faced each other across the kitchen table, Julia was already describing the scene to Michael. Either he would think it was funny, or he would say she was crazy. Madame Nora took Julia's hand and turned it palm up. She touched the inside of her wrist and lightly traced a blue vein into the palm. Then she pushed the little finger down and looked at the side of Julia's hand.

"I see one child," said Madame Nora.

Julia was surprised. She had always assumed that having several children was unavoidable. She glanced at the ceramic owl with a clock face on top of the refrigerator. It said three o'clock.

"Yes, you will live a long life," said Madame Nora.

Of course a palmist could not tell a client *soon you will die*, thought Julia.

"You have had trouble in your office and in your marriage."

"My office closed recently," Julia said. "I lost my job."

"That's what I mean," said the woman. "But don't believe what people say about him." She looked at Julia. "You are very temperamental, but you only get angry when you are right, never when you are wrong."

If anything, being wrong made Julia angry. What did people say about Michael?

"Soon you will get two letters, one good and the other bad. I don't mean tragic news, but a disappointment," said Madame Nora. "Know what I mean?"

Julia nodded. She knew she looked like a person who could not tolerate bad news. She often surprised herself looking faintly startled in mirrors. Her eyelashes were almost invisible from any distance at all.

"You are very determined," said the palmist. "You will not give up no matter how long it takes, but you do not yet have what you want. You will make friends more easily as you grow older."

"How long will it take to get what I want?"

"I cannot give you a time, but I see a man who helps you."

If she could be certain about the future, Julia thought, she would see herself differently in the present. The palmist coughed and said Thursday. Thursday was Julia's lucky day. She closed Julia's hand as if she were pressing a coin into the palm.

Julia walked up the block to the phone booth outside the grocery store on the corner. In the yellow pages she looked under *T* for TALENT AGENT. The listings went from TAILOR to TANK CLEAN- ING. She turned to *E* for ENTERTAINMENT.

"Where did you get that dress?" Lester Green stuck a cigarette between his teeth like a cigar and grimaced as he lit it.

Her dress was dark red and it was hand-tailored.

"Where did you get that jacket?" she said.

He was worse than she had imagined from the appearance of the building. He was gaunt, mustachioed, and wore a black-and-white checked jacket with winged lapels. His yellow hair was combed straight back. Lester Green was obviously not a person who cared about the classics.

"Mrs. Murphy," he said in a baritone voice. "What a name."

Julia laughed as if he had held up something ridiculous that did not belong to her. She was sitting on a metal folding chair in front of his tidy desk. On the floor not far from her feet was an unopened gallon of rosé wine.

"Ever done weddings, bar mitzvahs, anniversaries?" Lester Green leaned back and squinted.

The musty smell of the room reminded Julia of the apartment

where she had lived as a graduate student. She was trying to think of the name of the Italian bassist who lived below her. She said not really. It was Paul something.

"Do you belong to the musicians' federation?"

She shook her head again.

"You'll have to sign up," he said.

Julia looked out the window at a tarred roof across the alley.

"Tell me what you have done." Lester Green leaned forward. On the wall behind him was a photograph of himself as a young man in front of a microphone. The picture was autographed.

"I did my graduate studies in conducting and composition and I've taught piano lessons."

"Haven't you ever performed, Mrs. Murphy?"

"I've been working for a music publishing company," she said. "It went bankrupt."

"What was the name?"

"You've never heard of it." She told him the name.

"Never heard of it," he said. "Murphy. That's a god-awful name."

The phone rang and into it Lester Green said obscene words in combinations she had never heard before. So thin for such a deep voice. He slammed down the receiver.

"I don't want to be famous," she said.

"We all do," he said.

"I don't suppose I could be even if I wanted to." Julia looked at her hands.

"The fact is, you won't get famous and the odds are against making a dime in this piss-poor business. You're crazy to try. We're all crazy," he shouted.

His shouting relieved her and she was glad he put her in the company of others.

"Go down to the musicians' federation and fill out the forms," he said. "They'll want some money and an audition. Let's see how you sound." He pushed himself away from the desk.

An old black upright with cracked keys like dirty fingernails sat in the studio next to Lester Green's office. A slim electric guitar lay on top of a large amplifier. Lester Green leaned against the wall with his eyes closed as Julia sat down and struck a chord. The piano was more than a half-step off.

"Should I play anything in particular?" she said. She felt unreasonably nervous.

"Play what you like," he said without opening his eyes. He seemed settled into a silence that did not include her.

Julia began the slow minor tread of "Moonlight Sonata."

"Not that, please." He sighed.

She remembered a Duke Ellington number.

"That's it." Lester Green patted the top of the piano.

Julia improvised a little, wagging her shoulders, but she felt stiff. She closed her eyes and imagined a bass player behind her. When she opened her eyes again, Lester Green was dancing with the guitar. He was a beautiful dancer.

JULIA *visits the dentist*

Julia sat in a canvas deck chair next to an old woman wearing a beige cardigan over a pink dress. Another elderly woman sat across the waiting room. It was overheated.

"My dentures fit fine," said the woman next to Julia.

Julia smiled and picked up a copy of *Time* from the glass-topped table. On the walls were pictures of grinning, healthy-looking kids from different countries.

"Some people, their bottom teeth move up and down," said the woman.

Julia nodded.

"If you lose weight, your teeth move. My mother always had trouble with her teeth." The woman crossed her wrists over her stomach and picked at the wool of one sleeve.

Julia closed the magazine. "What time is your appointment?" she asked.

"Her appointment is at two-thirty," said the woman across the room.

Dr. Bornio had been recommended by friends. Even so, Julia did not know what she thought of a man who took a lot of elderly patients. Maybe he was after their Medicaid. Maybe he did unnecessary work. A third old woman had just come in. She sat slowly, her hands in the air grasping her two canes long after she had reached the chair.

"Have them pulled out and have decent ones put in," said the woman next to Julia. "You can't even budge mine." She tugged at her lower teeth with two fingers.

"We've been here since ten this morning," said the woman across the room. "We didn't know how long it would take to find his office."

"It is a little difficult to find," said Julia.

The receptionist slid open the office window and smiled around the room. "Mrs. Murphy?" she said.

Dr. Bornio was not black, as Julia had imagined from the sound of his name. He was a nice-looking young man who might have been on his college football team. He had fine, strong hands with little hair on them. The knuckles were large and the fingers long. They looked like sculptured hands Julia had seen in a museum. Dr. Bornio moved his thumb and index finger apart between her lips. Her mouth was open before she knew it.

Julia looked into his blue eyes. The irises had tiny spokes of gold. Toward the center the blue was pale. The center was where the eyes looked vulnerable; the iris was ringed by an icy shade of dark blue. Dr. Bornio's nose was sunburned and a little broad. His skin was shaved so closely, she could not see a sign of his beard. His breath smelled of clove and he wore a plaid sports shirt.

"Have you ever thought about getting rid of that little space between your front teeth?" he asked. He took the small metal instruments out of her mouth.

Of course she had thought about it. She shrugged.

"I don't think it would take much," he said.

"I'm too old for braces," said Julia.

"It's up to you," he said, putting the metal back into her mouth.

"A lot of adults get braces now. I could give you the name of an excellent orthodontist."

He moved behind her out of sight. Julia felt trapped behind the napkin around her neck and stared at the tray the assistant pulled in front of her chin. Beyond it on the wall was a photograph of a sailboat in blue-green water. It was anchored in a cove off a small island. The red roof of a villa showed through the dense trees that covered the island. Julia thought she had seen this place.

"Where was that picture taken?" she asked.

"In the Caribbean three years ago," he said behind her. "We used to go down there a lot, but it's gotten so darn crowded." He said something to the assistant who put a row of silver picks on the tray before Julia.

"I'm going to clean your teeth," said Dr. Bornio. "I always do it myself the first time."

Julia wanted to tell him that she had sailed in the Caribbean, too.

"Have you ever sailed?" His voice was raspy in her ear.

She raised her chin and looked into his eyes. He put a small mirror in the left corner of her mouth and a pick in the right.

"That's a mean trick, isn't it," he said. "Ask you a question and then put things in your mouth." He chuckled and began scraping the inside of her bottom front teeth. He told her about how once his mainsail had split down the middle in heavy winds. Julia tried to smile. She felt his body touching her arm. Once he rested his hand on her shoulder. He scraped and polished and scraped some more. Her gums felt injured. Finally, he raised the back of her chair and told her to rinse. The assistant went away.

Dr. Bornio folded his arms over his chest. He was not a tall man. He bit his upper lip with perfectly even lower teeth. "You're going to have to start flossing regularly, Julia," he said. He stared at her face. "That will keep the plaque from building up so fast."

Julia wanted to say something. She believed he was a good dentist. His hands were so fine.

"You also have a small filling that needs to be replaced." He lowered his head but kept his eyes on her face.

Julia saw them sailing in heavy winds, the boat heeling to port. She looked down at Charles from the starboard side and he smirked. He had those healthy teeth, but he had grown a beard.

"I'll make an appointment," Julia said.

"We'll see you soon then," he said. As he unfastened the chain to remove the napkin from around her neck, his hand stopped on her arm. Barely pressing, he squeezed. Julia couldn't move. She stared at the white yacht in the blue-green water.

JULIA *goes to a party*

"And so I ended up spending the summer in Arcachon," said Julia. "I lived with a family and took care of all the children. They were sweet and the whole summer was wonderful. The grandmother owned this huge beach house on the bay." She looked reminiscently into her glass of white wine.

The kids were insufferable brats. The adults quarreled incessantly. A divorce was brewing and the grandmother broke out with eczema. Julia, lonely and ashamed of her French, had gained ten pounds. Just before she left, the eldest son tried to molest her on a small sailboat practically in view of his wife who was sunbathing on the shore.

"That's how I learned my French, too," said the woman on the sofa next to Julia. "I spent two summers in France."

Across the room Michael was engrossed in talk with three men. The woman watched Julia closely.

"I think having a second language is essential," Julia said. "I was always sorry I didn't learn German as well."

"My Indonesian has certainly come in handy," said the woman.

"I'll bet it has," said Julia.

She excused herself to get another glass of wine. The host and hostess were standing by the sliding-glass doors to the garden, talking with a guest. Julia joined them and looked out at the brightly lit patio surrounded by a high brick wall.

It was raining.

"He served sparkling cider, no alcohol at all, and he played the piano. We were trapped," said Alice. "He was a horrible pianist. Not like you, Julia. She played for us last New Year's Eve," Alice said to the other woman. "It was very nice."

"I played for you last New Year's Eve?" said Julia.

"You didn't play with your hands, that's true," said the host.

"I remember sitting on the keyboard," said Julia.

"It was lovely," Alice insisted. Alice was elegant and pretty. She looked like a natural blond. "Anyway, he played the piano. We were forced to sit there and endure it with no alcohol to kill the pain." Her voice seemed about to break from fragility. Alice always talked this way.

"It was the worst thing I've ever been through," said the host.

"You were rude, dear," said Alice. "I was so embarrassed."

"Why are you crying?" Michael asked Julia on the way home.

"I don't remember," she said. The car seemed enormous inside. The glow from the radio was unearthly.

"I hate it when you drink so much," said Michael.

Julia looked at his profile in the radio light and wondered why she had married him.

"I had a horrible time," she said. "If you want someone to sit around parties and chat, you don't want me."

"I didn't say that."

"You implied it." Julia looked out at the passing street. It was black and slick-looking from the rain.

"I just hate it, that's all," said Michael. He did not look at her. He drove with both hands on top of the steering wheel.

"Well you hate me then," she said.

Michael parked in front of their house and walked to the door.

Julia saw disdain in his shoulders. She was furious that he didn't wait for her. She got out of the car, slammed the door hard, and marched up the walk.

"God damn you Michael," she screamed into the keyhole.

He opened the door.

"Cool it," he said. "Get in here."

Michael went upstairs. Julia took off her coat and threw it on the sofa. She went to the credenza, opened the door, and pulled out three crystal wine glasses. She threw them one by one against the wall. Julia loved her crystal. The sound of it shattering caused her pain. She took two more wine glasses and smashed them, and two more, two more, until she had broken eleven. Then she ran to the powder room and locked herself in. Michael was pounding on the door. She put a towel over her head and sat on the floor. She sobbed. She was in a deep dark hole.

JULIA *sees a psychiatrist*

As Julia stepped off the elevator, she wished someone else would go in her place. The endless corridor had shiny lemon walls. On the doors to her right were professional names in uniform gold lettering. The doors without names to her left were apartments, which explained the baked-fish smell. It was not the kind of building where she would run into any of her friends.

Dr. Bill Waters himself opened the door. She had chosen his name from the yellow pages because it did not call up any unpleasant images or memories. In person Dr. Waters did not remind her of anything unpleasant, either. His turtleneck sweater and trousers were light gray. He wore suede slippers. Julia took off her sunglasses and walked past him. The room was furnished with rust-and-brown striped chairs and a sofa. Yellow, dry-looking asparagus ferns hung in the window.

"Please sit wherever you like," said Dr. Waters.

Julia sat on the sofa.

"Are you comfortable?"

She wished she had chosen a chair. "This is fine," she said, looking him in the eye. He had large brown eyes. Eye contact was important in this situation, she thought.

He sat opposite her in a black swivel chair. "Do you mind if I take notes?" he asked. He combed his fingers through his thin hair. A yellow legal pad lay on his knees.

"Does anyone else see your notes?" she said, unable to look at him any longer.

"This is only to remind me of what we talk about," he said. "What can I do for you?"

Julia wished he had not put it that way. He sounded like a shoe salesman.

"I'm worried about myself lately," she said. "I'm thinking about having an affair, which is unlike me."

"That's interesting," he said. He moved his hand to his chin. "Why don't you?"

"What," she said.

"Have an affair."

"But I'm married." She folded her hands in her lap and thought of her mother.

"Why don't you think about how it might feel to have this affair, and explore those feelings?"

Julia looked at the way he was sitting with his legs crossed and his chin in one hand. "If I had one affair, it seems to me that I would be opening myself up to the possibility of more."

"You think having an affair would be wrong." He jotted down a few words. With his head bent, his face was at an attractive angle.

"Of course it would be wrong," said Julia. "But sometimes I get these wild urges."

"Tell me about them," said Dr. Waters.

Julia looked at her hands.

"Wild urges must make you feel out of control," he said.

"I went to this horrible man's office the other day," she said. "He's a talent agent. I was thinking of trying to get a job playing the piano in a gallery or at fashion shows. He asked me to play. I sat in front of this man and imagined myself playing in a piano bar. I've been picturing this scene ever since." Julia looked out the window at the blue, blue sky. "I was very good. The audience cried for encores."

"That's a touching fantasy," said Dr. Waters.

"What is so touching about it?" Julia felt like crying. "It isn't the first time I've imagined it. But it is the first time since my marriage that I've had the urge to go wild."

"You used to have this same fantasy."

"In college I was attracted to the low life." Julia laughed.

"Weren't we all," said Dr. Waters. "You said this talent agent was a horrible man."

"I only meant that he looks like a gangster. His office is over a dry cleaner."

"Why did you choose this talent agency?" asked Dr. Waters.

"I picked a name out of the phone book," she said.

"You don't think very much of your ability, do you," said Dr. Waters.

"You make me want to cry," she said, looking at the box of Kleenex on the coffee table.

"I don't think I make you want to cry," he said.

"Yes you do," she said.

"Is this talent agent the man you're interested in?"

Julia looked at Dr. Waters. He would like that, wouldn't he? That would make her very interesting.

"The man I am attracted to is my dentist," she said evenly. "He is a good dentist. He is also younger than I."

"How much younger," said Dr. Waters.

"He is perhaps thirty. I am thirty-five." She knew he would say she did not look it.

"You don't look it," he said.

Julia began to cry. She did not want Dr. Waters to see her cry. He leaned forward and pushed the box of Kleenex closer to her. She grabbed a handful. She had said too much.

"How is your relationship with your husband?" asked Dr. Waters.

"Michael and I almost never argue," she said.

"How is it in bed?"

Julia glared at the coffee table. How dare this man. "We've been married seven years, Dr. Waters," she said.

"I understand," he said.

"You do? What do you understand?"

"That you've been married seven years."

"I apologize," she said. She took more Kleenex and looked at the ferns in the window. "Why don't you water your plants," she said. "They'll die." The plants looked Oriental. She wished she were far away.

"I think we might have put our finger on something here," said Dr. Waters.

Julia loathed him for saying "we." She saw him look at his watch.

"Tell me about the other members of your family. Do you have children?"

"Not yet," she said. "I don't really want children."

"What about your parents. Any brothers or sisters?"

"My parents live in Ohio and I have a sister who is a filmmaker and travels quite a bit."

"How do you feel about your family?" he said.

"My folks are very nice people," she said. "But my sister and I fight every time we're together."

It bothered Julia now that Dr. Waters wore a matching turtleneck and trousers. She thought it was neurotic.

"Anger makes us feel separate," said Dr. Waters. "I have noticed this in myself."

"On the other hand," said Julia, "my sister and I can be close. I sometimes know what she is thinking."

Dr. Waters wrote something. "What is it about your sister that irritates you?" he asked.

"Jennifer is superficial. She wants to marry a man with money."

"Is she that different from you?"

Julia was annoyed. Michael's earning potential had only been a tiny consideration. She said nothing.

"You are wise to want to examine your feelings at this point in your life, Julia," said Dr. Waters. "Why don't we try to identify what you feel around your husband and see how that compares with the feelings you experienced toward your dentist."

"Your dentist" made her feel ridiculous.

"Try to be more aware of your feelings this week," he said.

"I am very aware of my feelings," said Julia.

JULIA *takes michael*
to a poetry seminar

Julia and Michael sat in the fourth row. Two rows down, a man took the rubber band off his ponytail and shook his long hair flirtatiously over his shoulders.

"Can everyone hear?" the poet asked from the stage. "I want everyone to hear the words." He tapped the microphone. "This mike is buzzing," he said with irritation. "Can someone fix this mike?" He looked offstage.

Michael shifted in the wooden seat beside Julia. "Jesus Christ," he said. "Who are these people?"

She wished he hadn't come. He was going to be angry when they got home. An offended-looking young man had just walked onstage with a guitar. He poured some hot tea into cups from a thermos and lit incense. Then he sat on a folding chair.

"Poetry is the method of a mind moving," the poet said.

He might not have been fat, Julia thought, looking at him now, a small, worried man in a dark suit. He wore a red shirt and silver tie. He might not have been swathed in white, either, she thought. The first time she saw him fifteen years ago, she had to stand on her books, the room was so crowded. He was sitting in the lotus position on the classroom floor. The man with him played finger cymbals.

The poet was talking about Kerouac's idea of spontaneous mind writing. Behind him on a pedestal sat a vase of red and yellow flowers. When he moved just so, the flowers seemed to be growing out of his head. Julia wondered if Michael saw it, too.

The poet looked out at them through his thick glasses. If they were fixed on a subject, he said, they would ignore rising thoughts and their writing would be strained. They wouldn't be representing their bodies.

Julia knew what Michael was thinking. "Being fixed on a subject was called concentration," he would say. She didn't look at him. The poet was advising them to practice awareness of awareness.

"Thoughts have form," he said. "Let them have their form, and let them go. Accumulate thought forms in a notebook."

"Thought forms?" Michael whispered.

"Use a fountain pen," said the poet, "not a ballpoint pen."

To clear their minds, they were going to meditate for seven minutes. They were to cover themselves with a veil of self-consciousness. At the end of seven minutes, each person was to compose a three-line poem.

"First thought, best thought," said the poet. "Don't stop to think of words, but try to see the picture better."

Julia tried to concentrate on her breathing, tracing it in and out with her imagination. Someone behind her moved and paper crinkled, deep like a grocery bag. She pulled her mind away from the sound. She listened to Michael's breathing.

Then, without warning, she saw her sister riding a tricycle. Jennifer was riding in circles in the middle of a busy intersection. She seemed to be looking for someone. Julia stood still beside the traffic signal. She couldn't move because the signal said DON'T WALK.

"Open your eyes slowly," said the poet. "Retain the three lines."

24

He asked a man in a leather hat to recite his three lines. The man said something about his car tires and their roundness. He was worried about them becoming unround. Next the poet called on the long-haired man two rows down. The man said his destiny was crashing on the shore. Gulls rose out of the crashing but the crashing was only crashing. The poet acted irritated. He said that didn't sound like raw thought. Then he pointed, his finger pecking the air, at Michael.

Julia felt sweaty. Michael stood up. No one else had stood.

"This place is an oven," Michael said in a clear voice. "It is a graveyard. It is a perfume shop." He sat down.

Julia stared straight ahead. No one laughed.

"What were you thinking before you said those lines?" Julia asked him on the way home. She looked out the window at the forms passing in the night.

"I was thinking the room was hot and the people looked like they'd gotten stuck in the sixties. But the incense was nice."

Then Julia remembered one of the poems she'd heard fifteen years ago. It was about sucking and licking. She was scared the police were going to come and drag her away because the poetry reading was an illegal activity. The poet had been banned from campus, but the liberals sneaked him on. For the occasion Julia had worn blue jeans, an Indian shirt, and old sandals.

JULIA *travels to visit her sister*

A tall man with a long chin leaned toward Julia over the reception desk. His thin arms stuck too far out of his shirt cuffs. "I would like to learn Chinese," he said, grinning as if he already knew too much about her.

"I've never taught it to adults," Julia said. She should have expected something like this, she thought. She asked for Jennifer's room number.

"Hey. I thought you were Jennifer," he said as she walked away.

"Everybody does," she said.

The man waiting for the elevator let her go in first. He wore a yellow windbreaker. She wondered why he was pretending to chew gum. Was he going to expose himself? She pressed *two*.

"I thought you were coming down last night," he said.

"I couldn't make it," said Julia. She didn't look at him.

"I played 'Melancholy Baby' for you."

"Can you play 'Blue Moon'?" she said.

"Come down tonight and I'll play it," he said.

She glanced at him. He had a sunburn and kept his hands in his jacket pockets.

"If I'm not too tired," she said.

Julia got off, expecting him to touch her shoulder. After the doors shut, she looked around. He wasn't there.

"You made it." Jennifer was younger than Julia but taller, and she wore outrageous clothes. Where had she gotten the nerve?

"Barely," said Julia. She put down her bag and sat in the chair by the window. The chair was dark green vinyl with metal arms. Voices went by outside the door. "How's the shoot going?" she asked.

"Crazy as usual," said Jennifer. She sat on the bed.

"A little craziness doesn't sound too bad," Julia said.

"Compared to what?" said Jennifer.

"Boredom."

"If you're unhappy, why don't you do something about it?"

"It isn't that easy," Julia said. "I lost my job."

"That isn't the reason you're unhappy," said Jennifer.

"How do you know?"

"I've never been married but I lived with someone."

Julia looked around. The carpet of Jennifer's room was thread-bare and the curtains were yellowed and lacy. In one corner was a sink and in another a metal desk. A single iron bed stood against one wall. The room looked like a nun's cell.

"You must be lonely," she said.

"I don't let myself feel lonely," said Jennifer.

"I do," said Julia.

Jennifer tilted her head to one side. "Sometimes I wonder if you give Michael a chance," she said.

Julia listened to the radiator clank. "This isn't why I came," she said.

Jennifer swung her legs off the bed. "I have to work this afternoon, but tonight we can talk. I'll have a rollaway sent up."

"Where are we going to put a rollaway?" Julia said.

After Jennifer left, Julia tried to read a paperback. She looked out the window at the main street below. They were in a small town. At home she had longed to talk to Jennifer about Michael, about life. But here, her instinct was to reveal nothing. At three she decided to catch the four o'clock bus home.

"Hey. I'd like to take you on a world cruise," the clerk said when Julia passed his desk.

She heard ice cubes being torn from a plastic tray in the kitchen as she walked in the front door. A stack of mail lay on the coffee table. For weeks she had waited for the two letters. Finally she quit waiting. Michael came out with a drink in his hand.

"You're back," he said. "I thought you were going to spend the night."

She shrugged. She did not want to talk about it. "What are these?" she said. There were two large boxes on the floor.

"Open them," he said.

Julia knelt and untied the string that had been made into a handle. Inside the box the things were wrapped separately in tissue paper. Michael turned on the television news but kept the volume low. Julia unwrapped a crystal wine glass in her wedding pattern.

"Oh Michael," she said. She unwrapped another. "How many are there?"

"Those eleven and then I thought I might as well finish out the set. You have all your red, white, and champagne now."

Julia stood and put her hands on his shoulders. He patted her back.

"Your mother will never find out," he said.

"I wasn't really worried about that," she said.

"Yes you were," he said.

JULIA *goes to a jazz club*

Julia sat on a stool and rested her feet on the rail at the base of the bar. The bartender was a short man with a paunch and white hair but a young face. He looked like the bartender she would have imagined if she had thought about it. He had protruding teeth that made his mouth too large, but friendly, when he smiled. A McCoy Tyner song was on the jukebox. Julia played the bar with one hand as if it were a piano.

"Do you play or are you just a listener?" the bartender asked. He was ringing up a bill on the cash register.

"I play the piano," she said.

"You ought to sign up for the jam session one afternoon," he said. His profile was lit by a small light clipped to the cash register.

"Maybe in a couple of years," she said.

He smiled at her. She could not tell if he was being nice or making fun. Julia concentrated on pouring beer into her glass. She rearranged her vest and purse on her lap and sipped the beer. She knew a tall black man was watching her in the mirror. He wore a leather jacket. She looked back at him. He touched his tongue to his upper lip.

"How are you this afternoon?" he said.

"Good," she said.

The man took his drink to the bandstand and sat down at the piano. The drummer, saxophonist, and bassist took their places. There was no crowd and the group started without an introduction. Julia kept time with her left foot. When the bartender looked at her empty bottle, she gave him a nod and he pulled another beer from the cooler. She had never felt such independence. He was running her a tab.

After the band finished that number, the pianist spoke in a hushed, menacing voice over the microphone. Julia did not catch his name. A group of women had crowded into the booth behind her. They were talking loudly about San Francisco.

"The man in the last booth asked if you would join him for a drink," the waitress said in Julia's ear.

"Oh, no thank you," said Julia. She had seen the man in the last booth. He was old-looking and wore a cowboy hat. What if he tapped her on the shoulder and pushed his bleary face into hers?

During the break the pianist walked past her again, his arm brushing her back. She thought about whether or not this could have been a signal. She peeled the label from her beer bottle and watched him. He talked to a lot of people but he did not act friendly. He seemed preoccupied. She wanted to know what preoccupied him.

"Excuse me, sir?" she heard herself say. Her voice seemed to come from the mirror. The black man looked down at her. She felt silly and inadequate, a small white woman with an L. L. Bean goose-down vest across her knees.

"Yes," he said, "what can I do for you?"

"Do you give piano lessons?" she said. Her stomach gnawed at her.

"Yes, I do," he said.

"Are you taking any new students?" she said.

"That depends on who the student is," he said.

"Me," she said. She introduced herself.

"Jolly Brown," he said.

"Jolly Brown," said Julia, "sounds like a name you made up." She laughed, wanting to apologize and start over. Jolly seemed to take up most of the space around them.

"It's a nice name," she went on. "I mean." She looked at the invisible marquee above him. "It would look great in lights."

Julia was sitting on the piano bench. Jolly had pulled a kitchen chair up to the keyboard. Around them every chair, table, and trunk was covered with piles of sheet music at least two feet high. An Indian blanket lay over the closed top of the grand piano.

"Let's get back to the real world," said Jolly.

Julia did not want to sleep with him, yet she felt that at any moment she would. She opened her thick songbook and played a Bill Evans tune she had practiced hundreds of times in preparation for this day. Technically, it went all right. But she felt almost no emotion. When she had finished, Jolly began leafing through the photocopied sheet music in a cardboard box on the floor.

"Was that improvised or had you worked it out in advance?" he said.

"I worked it out," she said.

"Let's try something you haven't practiced," he said, putting a sheet on the piano before her. She stared at his large brown hand. How could she show him she was more than she appeared to be?

It was a Duke Ellington song. To keep the rhythm going, Julia played simply through five choruses.

"I'm afraid you need a little more work before I can take you," said Jolly. "I'll recommend someone to get you in shape, if you want."

31

"How much do I need to learn?" she said.

"You'll know when you're ready. Don't worry."

Julia felt there must be some mistake. She always knew when she was going to get what she wanted, and Jolly had given her that feeling.

JULIA *tells michael she is*
seeing a psychiatrist

The street was still quiet. A patch of morning light fell on the rose-and-navy print wallpaper. Julia thought, I am going to watch that light. She knew the light would move as the sun rose and it would disappear. She looked at the long fingers of shadow that lay across the ceiling. The source of the shadow was the walnut tree outside their window.

Now the patch of light on the wall was gone. Julia regretted having missed it. She regretted it intensely and couldn't remember what she had been thinking that distracted her. She felt afraid. From the street came the roar of a car with a bad muffler.

Michael rolled over and hummed. His face was puffy and his hair stuck out all over. Even so, Michael was not unattractive. Julia counted the days since her last period. Twelve days. She got out of bed to go put in her diaphragm.

Back in bed she lay on her side with her back to Michael. She wanted him to hold her with his arms around her stomach so she would feel safe. She rubbed the sole of one foot up his shin, but he didn't move. He seemed to have fallen back asleep.

The air in the kitchen was chilly. Julia turned on the oven and opened the oven door. She stood in front of it, waiting for the water to boil. Michael would have a fit if he saw her using the stove to heat the room. The dog came into the kitchen, his nails clicking on the tile. He looked as if he needed something. Julia rubbed his ears and talked to him. Then she heard a thump overhead and, seconds later, the sound of the shower. She pulled a skillet from under the sink and turned on the small television on the counter.

"Coffee," Michael said. He was wearing a dark three-piece suit and his hair was washed and soft-looking, fine like baby's hair.

Julia poured him a cup, which he carried away. She heard the front door open and close. She moved the bacon around in the skillet. Michael came back into the kitchen with the paper.

"I don't have time to eat," he said.

"Breakfast is the most important meal of the day," she said, smiling to make him smile.

"All right." He frowned at the paper and quickly ate half the food she set before him.

After Michael left, Julia sat at the table with a cup of coffee and one of Michael's yellow legal pads. She drew a line down the center of the page. Above the left column she wrote CB for Charles Bornio and JB for Jolly Brown, and over the right she wrote MM. Under the CB/JB she listed eyes, skin, breath, hands, voice, light, color, silence. Under MM she wrote clock, time, closet, breakfast, hair, clothes, work.

Julia then drew another vertical line to divide the left column in two. Under the CB she wrote pretty, nervous, muddled, disappear. Under JB, afraid, awe, touch, try. Under MM she added small, apologetic, fault, clean house. She felt that Michael demanded perfection. She didn't think Jolly Brown would, but Charles Bornio might.

When Michael came home at seven, Julia told him she was seeing a psychiatrist. "Today was the third time," she said, poking at the fire to make the logs blaze again. When she turned around, Michael was watching her with small eyes. They got that way whenever she did anything unpredictable, she thought.

"Why in God's name would you go to a psychiatrist? You're not crazy."

He rested the hand with the cigarette in it on the couch. She wanted to tell him to move his hand so he would not burn a hole in the cushion. She closed the fireplace screen and sat in the wing chair opposite him. She felt small in the large chair.

"I've been depressed," she said. Her eyes filled with tears. "Life seems so flat." Julia had been both afraid and exhilarated by the idea of telling Michael. She had expected him to show concern.

"You're just depressed because of your job, babe," he said. "It isn't anything serious. I don't think you need a psychiatrist. Before you know it, you'll depend on the guy. How much does this cost?"

"Our insurance pays half."

Michael looked at the ceiling and shook his head. His mouth was pinched in that way she hated. It made his nose look too big.

"We can afford it, Michael," she said.

"But you don't need it," he said. "You're attractive and smart. A thousand women would give an arm or a leg to be in your shoes."

"Married to you?" She gave him a hard look.

"Being married to me isn't so bad, is it?" he said. He picked up his drink from the coffee table.

"Being married to you isn't always that great," she said and wished she hadn't.

"What are your major complaints?" He looked hurt.

"I don't know what they are." She wanted to fix herself another drink, but Michael would say she was drinking too much. She got up anyway and poured more Scotch into her glass.

"Look Michael," she said. "I'll just do it for a couple of months."

"Everybody feels depressed when they lose a job. Why don't you hunt for another job instead?"

"I'd like to try my luck at performing," she said.

"Why don't you get a normal job like other people?" he said. "Why don't you want a normal life?"

"Michael," she said. She wasn't like other people, she thought. "I have always, always wanted to perform. I would simply like to take advantage of this," she paused, "natural break. It is an opportunity." The room felt empty.

"I feel like you're changing the rules on me," he said. "You didn't mention any secret plan when we got married."

"You would support me if I had a baby."

"That's different." He lit another cigarette.

"You're killing yourself," she said. "I wish you would stop smoking."

"Get off my back."

"Why should I have a kid if my husband is going to die young?"

"You're getting drunk."

Julia threw the Scotch on him.

"God damn you," he said.

She went to the kitchen to get a rag to clean it up.

JULIA *attends a lecture*

"You look so reportorial," the young man said to Julia, leaning over the woman between them. The woman sat straight in her chair as if a spider were dropping on a thread before her. "Are you writing an article?" he said.

"I am not a reporter," Julia said. She crossed her legs and tossed the top foot several times. In her notebook she wrote lemons, cream, capers.

"Where do you live?" he asked.

She told him. "And you?"

"I'm moving to Cambridge," he said.

"When?" she said.

"In the fall," he said, "to teach at Harvard."

"That's wonderful," she said. She felt disappointed.

From the corner of her eye she could see his legs stretched out before him. He wore running shoes. When he pulled his legs back out of view and leaned forward, she told herself he was looking past her out the window, not at her. She shook her bangs away from her eyes and smiled at the woman next to her. The woman had white hair and her skin was still beautiful.

"I admire him so," the woman whispered, looking at the speaker who was walking to the podium. "This is going to be over my head."

Julia moved her hand away from her notebook. The movement seemed exaggerated, a mistake. Her arm might fly out of control. She wondered how she was going to make it to the door when the time came to leave.

Unnecessary notes break up the aesthetic wholeness and harmony, betray an uneasiness, she wrote. She guessed that the young man played bass. He would be no taller than his instrument. Unexpected notes can be witty, she wrote. His curly hair made him look witty. She felt him looking her way again. Was he or was he not really staring at her? she demanded of herself.

"Unexpected notes, where do they occur? Where do you put them?" the speaker asked.

Julia felt exquisite being watched. She kept her handwriting small. Does the organization reveal itself? she wrote and closed her notebook. She put the pen in her purse, took her jacket off the back of the chair, and slipped it on. She glanced at the young man. He smiled. She rushed from the room.

Julia strode through the rain toward her car. She felt extravagant, being so admired. She had walked three blocks when she tripped over a chunk of broken cement and her foot landed in a cold puddle. She began to run through the downpour. As she unlocked her car door, she saw clearly her embarrassing vanity. Inside the car, the air was chilly and damp. Something bad was going to happen to her. Carefully she started the engine and pulled away from the curb. She heard the wet street sizzle beneath her tires.

"I'd like to share a poem," a woman's voice said over the radio.

Julia slowed for a red light. Ahead, delivery trucks on both sides of the street had narrowed the traffic to one lane. She stopped in front of a tuxedo rental shop.

"Go ahead, share," said the announcer.

"Relationships," said the woman. "Give . . . love . . . forgive

. . . forgive. Communicate. Love . . . anger . . . understand . . . years . . . *years*. Give . . . self . . . other. Sensitive. Communicate. Share. *Love* . . . love. Thank you."

"Thank *you*," said the announcer. A commercial came on. The traffic started to move.

Julia stared at the radio. The car behind her honked as she pulled ahead. The traffic stopped and the light turned red again. Julia opened her notebook and wrote lemons, cream, capers. Capers, capers. Cream, lemons, lemons, butter. D'Anjou pears. Brie. Carr's water biscuits. Biscuits, lemons, cream. Anjou, Anjou.

JULIA *gives piano lessons*

Every time Julia shifted in the plush vinyl booth, air was expelled
from the cushion with a hiss that sounded like farting. The Reverend Benjamin Plough and his wife Sally sat side by side across
from her. Benjamin Plough looked well enough scrubbed and
mentally alert to be a surgeon. He took small bites and frequent
sips of iced tea. Julia had ordered boiled shrimp. Before Sally was
the fried captain's platter with a baked potato. Benjamin Plough,
a small, trim man, was having stuffed flounder for lunch.

"When did you say you and Sally went to Israel, Reverend
Plough?" said Julia. She dunked a small pink shrimp into the
horseradish sauce.

"Call me Ben, Julia," he said.

"Ben," she said.

Sally was digging into her fried fish with fingers and a fork.

"It was nineteen-sixty-five," he said.

"Sixty-six," said Sally. She had a pretty face.

"No, dear, it was sixty-five, two years before the war." He seemed
slightly rebellious.

Sally had been taking piano lessons from Julia for about two
months. Sometimes Julia drove to their house in the suburbs.

Sometimes Sally came to the Murphys' place in the city. Sally was very enthusiastic about her lessons.

"Jerusalem is beautiful," said Sally. "That was a wonderful time in our lives."

"I can't tell you how long I prayed for guidance on whether or not to go," said Ben. "When the fellowship came through, we realized our prayers had been answered." He did not take his eyes off Julia. "God works in mysterious ways," he said.

In 1965, Julia was a college freshman. She thought of Lonnie Davenport. "What did you do in Israel?" she said. Lonnie drove a baby-blue TR3. He went to class on a skateboard. Julia smiled.

"We lived on a kibbutz," said Sally. She had finished eating.

"I was working at the interdenominational center there," said Ben. "It had a marvelous library where I could do my research."

"What did you do on the kibbutz, Sally?" Julia said. She continued eating.

"Our oldest girl was a baby. I took care of her and worked in the nursery."

"That sounds like a wonderful experience," said Julia.

"Tell us about yourself," said Ben. He emphasized "your."

"I grew up on a farm in the Midwest," said Julia. This was not exactly true. Her cousins grew up on farms. There was a cornfield behind the subdivision where she grew up.

"A farm," said Ben. "That's fascinating." He crossed his knife and fork on his plate.

"I don't care much for city life," Julia said with annoyance. This wasn't true, either. She was still hungry but she stopped eating.

"That's too bad, since you live in the city," said Ben. He frowned.

The phone rang while Julia was balancing her checkbook. When she picked up the receiver, the caller hung up. Just as she sat down again at the kitchen table, the phone rang once more.

"It was I who called a moment ago," said Ben Plough in a small voice. "I was afraid to talk to you, so I hung up. Then I realized you might be frightened that it was an obscene caller, so I called back. I just wanted to know how you are, Julia." He sounded out of breath. "I saw you downtown the other day, but you were too far away."

"I appreciate your honesty, Ben," said Julia. She wanted him to know that she was not insensitive to anxiety and guilt. "Thank you for calling back." She did not want to go on, but she did. She asked him how he was.

"Sally is out of town, Julia," said Ben.

"I don't know what to say, Ben," she said.

"I think about you, Julia," said Ben.

Julia was silent.

"I have thoughts I shouldn't have," Ben said.

"I know what you mean," said Julia.

"Do you?" he said.

"When it happened to me, I went to see a psychiatrist."

"What did he say?"

"He told me to think about it and explore the feelings."

"I can't do that," Ben said.

"I guess it would be better if you didn't," she said.

"You won't mention this phone call to Sally," he said.

"Of course not," said Julia. "My lips are sealed."

"He thinks so little of himself," said Sally. "I've never been able to bolster his self-image." She smiled brightly at Julia across the table. "He plays racquetball twice a week. Maybe it's someone at his club."

Sally's fettuccine arrived. Julia was having endive salad.

"I wish I were as thin as you are," said Sally. "I guess I need more energy or something. Anyway, I don't mean a sexual affair. What I'm talking about is an affair of the mind."

Julia was wiping salad dressing off her silk blouse.

"He's been so happy and distracted lately," said Sally. She sighed.
"You don't seem too upset," said Julia.

"I had one of those little affairs once," said Sally. "It meant the world to me. When I look back on it, I think Sally, you could have lived without that. But at the time, it was something."

JULIA *interviews for a job*

"What does this mean?" said Julia. "A challenging growth opportunity in an administrative/executive-assistant position that calls for supervisory, organizational, and interpersonal skills." She looked at the single daisy in the cut-glass vase on Betsy Flower's desk.

"That's a sample of language you might use on your résumé,"said Betsy, "if you want to work in an office and move into management." She wore a dusty-rose ultrasuede suit with the jacket collar turned up. She seemed unable to turn her head.

"I'm a musician," said Julia. "I only want temporary work to make some extra money."

"You should have gone to a temporary agency." Betsy touched an index finger to her tongue and flipped through more pages of a loose-leaf notebook.

"As a pianist, I type rather well," said Julia.

Betsy looked up but directed her eyes to a spot behind Julia as if a more promising client stood there.

"My husband uses this agency," said Julia. She shifted in her chair. She hadn't wanted to bring up Michael, even though he told her to take advantage of his connections. "His name is Michael Murphy," she said.

Betsy covered her cheeks with her fingers. The nails were long and deep rose. "You're Michael Murphy's wife? I know him very well. We're dear, old friends." Her voice dropped an octave. "I've been telling him for months how much I would like to meet you."

"You have," said Julia. "Nice to meet you."

"It's almost noon. Would you like to go out for lunch?"

On the wall behind Betsy was a color photograph of a ski lodge. Skis and poles stuck out of the snow everywhere and there were several picnic tables lined with people in parkas and sunglasses. Julia thought she had been to this place.

"I'm sorry," she said, lowering her voice to match Betsy's, "but I have an appointment with my psychiatrist."

"Oh," said Betsy. She blinked. "Perhaps another day then. Do you get downtown often?"

"No," said Julia. "Only on the days I see my psychiatrist."

"I see," said Betsy.

"This is a writing position," said Harold Kramer. "I don't understand why Betsy sent you over." Behind him, three stone Buddhas sat on a low credenza.

"I wrote biographical sketches of musicians, in my old job," said Julia.

"Then you should have brought writing samples," he said.

Harold Kramer looked too thick for his suit. He had wavy brown hair and a fat nose. He appeared sleepy. He had pulled his chair out from behind the desk so that he and Julia sat facing each other with nothing between them. Three inches of hairy white leg showed between his pants cuff and black sock.

"Have you done any other writing?" he said, pressing his fingertips together in front of his face.

"Not really," she said. She was thinking he would be awkward in bed.

"What books do you read?" he asked.

"Lately I've been reading a lot of Doris Lessing," said Julia.

"Ah. My wife went through a period when she read Doris Lessing. *Four-Gated City* or something, wasn't it?" He recrossed his legs and shifted onto his other big thigh.

Julia watched his thigh. She did not trust a man who knew the titles of women's literature.

"What do you do in your spare time?" he asked, not unpleasantly.

"I play the piano," said Julia. She smiled as blankly as possible.

"Ah," he said, looking at the ceiling. "That's fine."

"What do you do in your spare time?" she said.

He cleared his throat. "I, my family, that is, we ski and sail. I trout fish with my boy. He's quite a tennis player, too."

"How many children do you have?" Julia asked.

"I have three. The two older girls are away at college, in New Orleans, and the boy goes to private school. Yes."

"It sounds like a nice family. And your wife?"

"She's writing her third cookbook now."

"Oh my," said Julia.

"Well, Mrs. Murphy," he said, getting up. "I wish I could give you more hope, but it seems your qualifications don't meet our requirements. You see what I mean."

"That's perfectly all right, Mr. Kramer," Julia said, rising. She held out her hand. "You're a nice man. Don't worry about a thing."

"You told her you're seeing a psychiatrist?" Michael said. He lit a cigarette.

"I don't know why I said it. You should have seen the look on her face." Julia checked the potatoes boiling on the stove.

"I'll bet," said Michael.

"Come on," said Julia.

"I don't want Betsy knowing our personal business."

"Why was that Aspen ski picture on her wall?" Julia turned to him. "Michael. What was it doing there? Tell me."

Michael smiled slightly as if remembering himself in a terrific moment. "When she moved into that office, her walls were bare."

"Her walls were bare," Julia said. "Her walls were bare."

"We're good friends. I met Betsy working on the campaign."

"Her face turned bright red at the sound of your name, Michael," said Julia. Her eyes were burning.

"Oh Jesus," said Michael. He looked at the pot on the stove.

"You can't deny it now, can you? She was in Kansas City, wasn't she? And Boise. I knew something was going on." Julia began to cry. "Don't touch me," she said.

She closed her eyes and pressed her fists to her mouth. Here life was at last.

JULIA *decides to get rid of dr. waters*

Michael's shoe in the plank of morning light before the door closed was the last she saw of him. Julia poured another cup of coffee and sat back down at the kitchen table. She imagined Michael's relief as he stepped into the outside world.

Perhaps she should get rid of Dr. Waters, she thought. He never told her what to do about any of this. "You feel that he is evasive," he would say. "This is your feeling, not his." She wanted someone to shake her up. Dr. Waters never even criticized her; he was too nice. She was nostalgic for nasty feelings.

"Dr. Waters," she would say, "I'm going to stop coming for a while. I need to straighten things out in my mind."

"Julia," he would say, "let me in on your thoughts. Try and get at the feeling." She was sick of these phrases.

"Dr. Waters. Michael and I are going to Europe. I'll call you when we get back."

"Call me when you get back, Julia."

"Frankly, Dr. Waters, I don't think we're getting anywhere. Talking to you is like talking to a tape recorder."

She felt better.

"Furthermore, Dr. Waters, I think you have problems of your own. You're too passive."

Julia looked out the window at the patio. A bright cardinal sat in the heart of an azalea bush. "And Dr. Waters, I don't think it takes more than weekend training to be able to repeat everything someone says to you. You're like a mirror. I grimace, you grimace." She knew Dr. Waters was unmarried and that his mother and brother lived far away, in Seattle. But sometimes she felt she was the only person alive in the room.

Something thudded against the front door and Julia got up. It sounded like the newspaper. Michael had been irritated with nothing to read over his cereal. They had barely spoken to each other. Julia went to the door and opened it wide. The thin delivery boy was getting on his bicycle. Like a spider, he bent over the handlebars and grinned at her. Julia grabbed the top of her nightgown, whisked the paper off the step, and backed inside. She stood with her back against the locked door, her heart pounding.

JULIA *and michael go to france*

The black-and-white Norman cow was vibrating. Julia asked Michael to turn off the engine. She steadied the camera on top of the Le Car.

"It looks like an ordinary cow," said Michael.

"Look at the stone farmhouse. Look at that barn. Just look at them," said Julia. Through the viewfinder the scene lost some of its quaintness, but she took the picture anyway.

"This is the last time I'm stopping for cows, Julia," Michael said as she got back into the car.

"How many war memorials are we going to inspect?" she said. They lurched forward.

In Forges-les-Eaux, Michael parked in front of the World War II monument. Julia translated part of the epitaph out loud. Michael sat with his eyes closed, his arms over the steering wheel. She did not understand his fascination with the war. He probably imagined himself a speck falling into a purple dawn behind Allied lines. Julia wondered how he would have felt, leaving her behind in America to work in some factory.

From Forges-les-Eaux they drove north through more dairy country to Eawy Forest. The road numbers in the forest did not seem real. Michael followed D 118, a narrow asphalt road leading into the trees. Julia had the feeling they were entering a place that would change them. D 118 turned into a dirt lane. Michael stopped the car. Under the canopy of leaves, the air was yellow and smelled damp. Without speaking, they got out and started up a footpath crossed by a bridle trail. Julia spotted fresh hoofprints. They walked on until Michael stopped.

"This is far enough," he said. "Lie down."

Julia sat on the cool ground. The forest was quiet. Michael knelt, snapping a twig. It sounded like an explosion. He moved toward her and stopped with his lips barely touching hers, breathing into her mouth. She put her arms around his neck. He raised his head and listened. She heard a car somewhere far away.

"It's okay, Michael," she said.

"It's no good," he said. "I'm too nervous." He stood up and walked over to a tree and took a piss. He said he wanted to find the fastest way to Omaha Beach. He was tired of dicking around in the country.

On the coastal road to Fécamp, Michael showed Julia her first pillbox. It was in a green field above a chalk cliff beside the Atlantic. Michael walked in and out of the pillbox, examining the huge gun that protruded from it. Julia took close-up pictures of tiny yellow and purple flowers in the coarse grass. She lay on her stomach at the very edge of the cliff and sighted along it down the beach. Chalk dust blew in her face. Far below, nude bathers lay in the sun. Julia took pictures of them with her telephoto lens.

By the time they got to Le Hoc Point, it was raining hard. Michael said this was good because it would help them imagine how difficult the operation had been. There was a terrible storm before D-Day.

"Think about trying to climb a rope up that mother with Germans firing down on you," said Michael. He made his lips thin.

Julia didn't like Michael to tell her what to think, but she looked over the cliff. "Why would they even try it?" she said. She was shivering. The wind whipped the rain under her umbrella.

"They had to try and knock out that big German gun on top," said Michael. "Finally, the Americans called in shellfire from the U.S.S. *Texas*."

"You mean, we fired on our own men?"

"We had to."

"No we didn't," said Julia. She started back toward the car.

That night in the Hôtel de la Plage on Omaha Beach, Julia dreamed that she was on the beach in Normandy when the men landed. She escaped the Germans with an American soldier and they hid in an abandoned farmhouse. They became lovers in the attic. He was Michael and then he was a stranger. She was herself and then she wasn't.

In the middle of her *crabe à la mayonnaise*, the man at the next table said something. Julia looked at him. He was going bald but he had a nice smile.

"*Avez-vous jamais vu la Tunisie?*" he asked.

She said no. She did not know if she was up to a conversation. Michael had just left for Brussels on business.

"Tunisia is a beautiful country," he said. "I was born in Tunisia."

Julia had more than half her crab salad to go. She looked at it and at the man. He was on coffee. There were only a few patrons left in the sidewalk café. He did not seem to want to join her and it embarrassed her to talk from table to table as if she were getting picked up. He spoke quickly in French again. He said he was a dentist and that he was sending money back to his mother in Tunisia. He told other details Julia could not understand. His name was William something. He handed her a card: Guillaume Bourbet. There was a phone number under the name.

"Would you have dinner with me tonight?" he said.

So. She was getting picked up. She didn't see the harm. She

would meet him at the restaurant. He told her nine o'clock and gave her the address of an Italian place on the Left Bank. Then he said he had to go back to work. The whole conversation had taken only ten minutes. She had not even finished her crab salad.

From her hotel later in the afternoon, Julia called the number. A woman answered. Julia asked to speak to Guillaume Bourbet, *le dentiste.* The woman said *ne quittez pas.* He was, then, a dentist. When his voice came over the phone, Julia was surprised that she recognized it. She felt close to him and was glad they were going to meet. She said she would be a little late, but she would be there. He sounded in a hurry.

"I sang in nightclubs as a student," he told her. They were sitting at a table next to five noisy Americans who were complaining about everything. Julia asked William to speak to her in French. He had also done theater work, he said, though she didn't understand much of what he told her about it. He said he had talent. Julia had noticed the same ability in other French people to describe themselves with confidence. She asked William to order for her. It made her feel she was being taken care of.

"Let's walk," he said after coffee.

She said all right. She was up for anything. She tried to explain the word "up." Happy, enthusiastic, agreeable. His English was better than her French. When the bill came, Julia wanted to pay her share but William insisted. "*Mais ta mère, ta mère,*" she said. He seemed not to understand.

They walked without conversation in a soft rain for several blocks. The lights from the *tabacs* and cafés lit the wet cement before them. Then William began to sing to her in a low bistro voice. She was enchanted. William was not exactly the right person, but she was enjoying herself.

"My car is near," he said.

"Your car?" she said.

He turned an imaginary steering wheel in the air.

William drove his small car very fast through the glistening streets of Paris. Julia leaned her head back and inhaled the smoke from his Gauloise. She felt like laughing, she was so happy. She watched his profile in the glow of the dashboard lights. He stopped the car in front of an old building.

"Here is my apartment," he said. "We can have one drink."

She did not want to go into his apartment but she said okay.

His apartment was sparsely furnished with homemade furniture. He must have plenty of money to send his mother, thought Julia, living in such a place. He showed her a coffee table he had just finished. The wood was splintery. He told Julia to sit down and asked her what she wanted to drink. He began rifling around in an old cabinet.

"*Un petit peu de whisky,*" she said. At least she could practice her French.

"Have you ever seen anything like this?" he asked, opening a magazine before her. On the right page was a picture of a woman putting a carrot inside her vagina. He turned the page to pictures of other women, other vegetables.

"I have never seen anything like this," she said. She stood up.

William kissed her lightly on the mouth. Then he put his arms around her and kissed her hard, breathing noisily, as if they had already been kissing for some time.

"I have to go," Julia said. "*L'hôtel, l'hôtel.*" She was frightened. He stood between her and the door. Together they moved toward it. She could not think of how to ask for a taxi in French. At the door he kissed her again, violently. Julia was afraid to push him away. The room was so cold.

"Americans are afraid to be happy," William told her in the car. He continued in French. She understood only part of it. He said Americans avoided any opportunity for *la spontanéité*. She understood that, *la spontanéité*.

"I am sorry," Julia said when they reached her hotel. She spoke slowly so he would not be confused. "I am married. In America, marriage is happy. I am happy. I did not mean to suggest by going out with you that I am unhappy." Finally she got out of his car.

JULIA *calls the police*

If he hadn't arrived in a noisy yellow slicker, she would have felt safer. The young officer looked like an enormous schoolboy. When he spoke, Julia could tell he came from Brooklyn. His name was Al Sapreto. Lieutenant Sapreto looked without expression at Julia as if he knew he had tracked on the Persian rug. His shoes were large, black, and beaded with rain. There was not a crease or worry wrinkle on his round, placid face.

"Please sit down, Al," Julia said as they entered the living room. The fire popped. His slicker crinkled loudly when he sat. Julia took the Victorian wing chair across from him. She looked at the fire.

"Sorry it took me so long to get here," said Lieutenant Sapreto.

"There was no hurry," she said.

"Let me get my pad and pencil so I can write everything down," he said. He dug around inside his slicker and pulled out a small black notebook which he flopped open on his knee. He poised his right hand to write.

"I got home at seven-thirty last night," she said. "But I didn't notice anything then."

Lieutenant Sapreto rested his right hand on his thigh.

"This morning I went into the guest room for something and

saw that the bed had been slept in during our absence. We were in Europe for two weeks."

"Anybody know you were gone?"

"Our neighbor watered the plants," she said.

Lieutenant Sapreto looked between the pad and the coffee table several times, not writing. He stared at the ashtray.

"Would you like to smoke?" said Julia.

"No thanks. I don't smoke," he said.

"I did find Marlboro cigarette butts in the guest room. My husband smokes Winston Lights," she said. "There was a strange brown-and-white sheet stuffed under the bed and I found a pair of boys' underwear in the closet. They were size sixteen. My husband wears a thirty-two."

Lieutenant Sapreto rubbed his chin. "We had a lady with the same thing not too long ago," he said. "She lives on Elm past the Chinese take-out. Know where I mean?"

Julia shook her head. She didn't care about the other woman.

"Boys' underwear, the whole bit. Somebody leaves town and the kids use their house for parties."

"They mustn't think they can get away with it," said Julia. She stood up.

"This kid must be running low on underwear, if you know what I mean," said Lieutenant Sapreto. He laughed, then cleared his throat and asked her if she had a key hidden outside.

She realized it was a terrible mistake to do that, she said, and told him where.

"That's the first place they look," he said, shaking his head. He wrote it down and asked her if anything was missing.

"Not really. Some beer," she said.

Lieutenant Sapreto leaned back in the chair. "There isn't much we can do if nothing valuable is missing," he said. "I can write it up. That's about all."

Julia took the poker and jabbed at the burning logs. She put another log on the fire. Close to the hearth, her face got hot. She watched the coals pulse. Those youngsters had sex in her house. To preserve the evidence she had not washed the sheets. She had put the strange toothbrush in a plastic Baggie. She had picked cigarette butts out of the garbage and crawled under the baby grand to collect the pistachio shells. She stood and faced the lieutenant.

"Don't worry, Mrs. Murphy," he said. "We'll try to get to the bottom of this." He closed his notebook.

Julia walked him to the front door, wanting to detain him, but she could think of nothing further to say.

"Do you want to press charges if we find those kids?" Lieutenant Sapreto asked.

"I'll have to talk that over with Mr. Murphy," she said, wondering why she had called Michael "Mr. Murphy." Julia opened the door and she and Lieutenant Sapreto looked outside at the rain.

"Nasty night," he said.

She shut the door after him and leaned her forehead against it. The wood was cool. She could smell the fireplace smoking a little and she heard the dog hop down off the bed upstairs. Some people would say she was overreacting, calling the police on those kids.

JULIA *sees michael's ex-wife on the street*

"I saw your ex-wife on the street today," Julia said. She turned from the window where she was watching the rain. The night outside was vast, black, and shiny. Michael was trying to build a fire, but the kindling was wet. "I saw her coming out of Elizabeth Arden's, three blocks from your office."

"I know."

"You know what?"

"That she's in town. She's been dating a guy she met at the wedding."

"Why didn't you tell me?" said Julia.

Michael looked at her from his kneeling position. "Shit," he said. "I can't get this started." He glowered at the fireplace.

"Michael, why didn't you tell me?" Julia pressed her back against the cold glass.

"Look babe," he said, standing up. He held his hands before him as if he were asking her for something. "I didn't think there was any use in getting you upset if nothing was going to come of it. I see that was a mistake. I admit it."

"When are you going to start treating me like a wife and tell me things? I get so hurt sometimes."

"I was trying not to hurt you."

"Do me a favor and don't try not to hurt me," she said. She wanted him to come to her and hold her, but she wasn't going to ask him. Her arms hung limp at her sides. Michael sat on the sofa and scratched his head.

"I tried to do the right thing," he said.

"But you didn't," she said.

"Julia. I think Anna's moving here to live with this guy."

"You'd like to have her back, wouldn't you."

"I married you, for God's sake."

"You married me because I asked you to," she said. "Why did I do that?" She pushed her hair back and held her forehead.

When she was eight, she had made a sign for car trips. The sign read HELP! I'M BEING KIDNAPPED. She held it up whenever a car passed.

"Do you think you made a mistake?" said Michael.

Julia had never thought herself capable of such a mistake.

"Why did you let me think you loved me?" she said at last.

As she went out the door, Michael said he did love her. But she didn't believe him. She had never believed any of the people who said they loved her. She walked to the corner and headed toward the park. The streetlights were blurry in the rain. Her hair was sticking to her head. Tears and water streamed down her face.

Lieutenant Sapreto came to the house again in his yellow slicker. "Why did you even speak to the man?" Michael was asking.

Julia shrugged. She did not want to tell them that she didn't want to appear discourteous, even to a stranger in the rain.

Lieutenant Sapreto took a few notes. "I'll file a complaint," he said. "This description could fit a hundred guys, but we'll see what turns up."

"Do you think he would have hurt me?" Julia said.

"I don't want to scare you, Mrs. Murphy," he said, "but he was probably going to drag you off to those restrooms at the end of the park." He put on his plastic-covered hat before going back out into the rain.

Julia was relieved that he had confirmed the danger; otherwise, she might not have believed it herself. She could hear what other people would say. He only exposed himself? That happens all the time. Julia would have to tell them what Lieutenant Sapreto said. Besides, the man had touched her, which made it assault.

Michael had gotten the fire started. Her hair was nearly dry.

"I didn't like you running off like that," he said.

"You could have stopped me," she said.

"I was too damn mad," he said. "And I'm not going to tell you how to live your life."

"I wouldn't mind it if, now and then, you told me what to do," she said.

"Don't ever do that again," he said. He squinted at her as if she were too bright.

JULIA *finds a new therapist*

"I was assaulted last week but that's not why I'm here."

"I'm looking forward to hearing why you're here," said Albert Purser.

Julia had chosen his name from the yellow pages on the basis of his address, which was the farthest possible from Dr. Waters. Albert saw clients at his house. He had asked her to call him Albert.

"I'm making some ginseng tea." Albert clapped his hands. "Want some?"

"Isn't that a drug?" she said. In this room she thought she would feel freer to be herself than in most places. It was furnished with rugs and pillows. Large windows overlooked a creek.

Albert laughed. "It's an ancient Chinese remedy. Unless you drink too much, then you get diarrhea. I know." He disappeared into the kitchen and came back with one cup.

Julia settled herself on a floor pillow. Next time she would wear jeans.

"Sure you won't have some?" he said, bending but not sitting.

"Maybe I will," she said.

"That a girl," he said.

The tea tasted slightly of dirt, but she said it was delicious. Albert sat on a large pillow opposite her. He was a disheveled young man. She looked him in the eye.

"I'm here to switch therapists."

"How did you find me?"

She told him.

"This is great stuff," he said. He rubbed the back of his neck and grimaced.

"I started therapy almost three months ago because I wanted to have an affair. My husband and I hardly ever fought, life was fairly smooth. Dull but smooth. Now we fight a lot and I'm upset all the time. I want you to tell me why."

"I will if I can."

"You don't know what a relief it is to hear a definitive statement."

"Have you had an affair?"

"No, but I might. I'm bored to death with Michael," she said. "We only have sex twice a month and we never talk about anything important." It sounded worse than she had thought.

"You really care about this guy?" he asked.

"I never thought about not caring."

"You're an attractive woman. You don't have to put up with a lot of shit if you don't want to. You could find some other guy."

"I imagine I could," she said.

"Do you have a lot of women friends?" he asked.

"Not really," she said.

Albert stared at her. She did not know what he expected her to do. His eyes seemed empty, in need of filling. She moved her hand slightly toward him. In a few more seconds he would reach out to her and they would hold hands. Must she look at him as long as he looked at her? Julia squinted at the window and glanced about the room. His eyes were the trap.

"Julia, look at me," he said.

"I can't," she whispered.

"Why don't you have any friends?"

"Most people don't interest me very much."

"I have a hunch you're scared. Do you know that?"

"I've never been scared before," she said, looking at him.

"You're very hungry."

"I'm not scared and I'm not hungry," she said quickly. The situation had become dangerous. She wanted to fall into his arms.

JULIA *and jennifer go back to their hometown*

"You guys," said Dorothy. She clamped her hand over her mouth. "I didn't think you'd be here so soon."

"Surprise," said Julia. She noticed Dorothy was still biting her nails.

Dorothy touched her wet hair. "I wanted to look good, but here you are."

"I love your house," said Jennifer.

Julia walked into the living room. Dorothy's furniture would look good in a psychiatrist's office, she thought. Dorothy and Jennifer came in with their arms around each other.

"How old are your kids?" said Julia.

"They're such big neat kids," said Dorothy. "They're fifteen, twelve, and nine. Hey, I'm sorry to hear about your grandmother."

"She's too stubborn to die," said Julia. She frowned out the window. In the backyard was a tractor tire full of sand.

"You two haven't changed a bit," Dorothy said.

She and Jennifer sat on one sofa and Julia sat facing them in a matching chair. Jennifer poured wine into the glasses on the coffee table. Dorothy had gotten out her crystal.

"We just saw Marty Farmer at the drugstore," said Jennifer. "What happened to her?"

"She got pregnant and married Chuck Lovall," said Dorothy.

"Chuck Lovall," said Julia. "He was my boyfriend in sixth grade."

"She ran away with an older man a year later and left the baby with her folks," said Dorothy. "She's made it hard on herself."

"She looks it," said Jennifer.

"We weren't allowed to stand by the magazine rack at the drugstore," said Julia.

"I heard her brother went to Hollywood," Jennifer said.

"He was in a couple of Westerns." Dorothy covered her face. "They were awful."

"How's Nick?" said Julia.

"He's just great," said Dorothy. She leaned forward to pour herself more wine. "I mean, when you're married to a man for sixteen years, he better be great."

"Has he had any affairs?" said Jennifer.

"You don't have to answer that," said Julia.

Jennifer pulled one leg up under her on the couch. "I just want to know what life is like in a small town," she said.

"You big-city guys," said Dorothy, "I really envy you."

"Well don't," said Jennifer.

"A neighbor called me after I had Sammy," said Dorothy. "She said a girl had been going in and out of our house the whole time I was in the hospital. I was too tired to care then, but occasionally I wonder if he was having an affair."

"It could have been a sitter," said Julia.

"Why don't you ask him?" said Jennifer.

"I'd rather not know. I don't know why I'm telling you guys this. I never told anyone else," Dorothy said.

"The man I lived with had an affair," said Jennifer.

Julia had never heard this. She felt hurt.

66

"Don't feel like the Lone Ranger," said Dorothy. "I can't tell you how many people have told me the same thing."

"When I found out, I took everything good and left."

"When you're married and have kids, you don't have as many options," Dorothy said. "Besides, I'm pretty crazy about Nick."

"I was crazy about Patrick, too. I went to a therapist."

Julia had heard this part of it. She waited to see if Jennifer would tell it the same way.

"Mom suggested it, of all people. She thought I was a wreck. This shrink spent the hour telling me his troubles. I couldn't wait to get out of there."

The story hadn't changed. Julia looked at them looking at her. "Michael has never had an affair that I know of," she said.

Nick walked in the front door and slammed it. Julia stopped breathing. He seemed not to have changed at all. He was still muscular and young-looking. His jeans were tight and faded. She looked at his face. He was watching her.

"Hey," Jennifer shouted. She jumped up.

Julia got up, too, and went to him. Nick put one arm around Jennifer and the other around her. Julia inhaled the smell of his damp T-shirt. He seemed like an old lover. Jennifer said something to him and he laughed, then he turned to Julia.

"We're sorry to hear about your grandmother," he said.

"She couldn't possibly live alone now," said Julia. "One day she left the gas on and nearly blew herself up." No one laughed. If they knew how she felt with Nick's arm around her, they would think she was awful.

When Julia saw her grandmother, she started to cry. Not that Julia had ever liked her grandmother much. But the old woman could not even get out of bed and the room smelled bad. Her withered roommate lay staring at Julia. The curtains were closed making the room almost dark.

"It's Julia, Grandmother," she said. Julia cranked up the head of the bed and put her grandmother's glasses on her. "Remember me?" she said, putting her face close.

"I don't believe I do," said her grandmother.

"You remember Julia and Jennifer," said Julia.

"Now I remember," said the old woman. She spoke in a singsong voice that sounded untruthful.

"Jennifer had to fly to Europe," said Julia. She flapped her hands. "She flew to Europe."

"I remember," said her grandmother.

Julia rang for an attendant to have her grandmother put in a wheelchair. The fat young woman talked loudly as she strapped her into the chair. Julia told herself the harness was necessary even though it looked cruel. She vowed she would never get old like this. More exercise. Better diet.

Julia smiled at the ladies in the hallway as she pushed her grandmother along. They lined the walls, small and hunched over in nightgowns with faded designs. When she got home, maybe she would visit a convalescent home, she thought. She could start a music program and conduct singing one afternoon a week. Old people would probably want to sing hymns.

"Are you thirsty?" Julia asked.

"Yes," her grandmother said, smiling blankly.

Never had the old lady been so docile. Julia got an orange soda and a cola out of a refreshment machine in the lounge. She also bought a bag of cheese crackers. A nurse's aide stopped and patted her grandmother on the arm.

"She's a sweetie," she said. "A favorite around here. You should see some of them." She went away.

"What did you do this morning?" Julia said as she opened the crackers.

"I couldn't say," said her grandmother.

Julia held out a cracker and the old woman nibbled at it as if it were just out of reach. Julia pushed it into her mouth. More teeth were missing. She remembered how plump her grandmother used to be and how she played the piano and sang with true gusto. Gertie sometimes made them get up in front of the congregation of her church and sing "Jesus Loves Me." It was torture.

"I just saw Dorothy and Nick. Remember Dorothy used to walk us to your house after school?" Her grandmother would not let Dorothy into the house because she was a Catholic.

"No, I don't believe I do."

"Do you remember Oscar and Lillian? They're my mother and father. Oscar is your son."

"I don't trust them," her grandmother said.

Julia tried to give her a drink. "Don't you like Pepsi anymore, Grandmother?"

"It's too strong."

Julia opened the orange soda. "Can you still name the presidents of the United States?" she said. "Start with Washington."

Her grandmother said them all up to Teddy Roosevelt. She spoke in her light, untruthful voice.

"That's very good, Grandmother," said Julia. She held the old woman's hand. It was almost weightless. She tried to find her own features in her grandmother's face. She was going to look like her grandmother. Her eyes would become smaller, slanted, and unseeing. Her nose and ears would never stop growing.

Countless nights Julia had awakened in her grandparents' house to the sounds of traffic outside, the walls moving with light, and the night exotic from the smell of potted violets. She tried to stay awake. The next moment she smelled bacon frying and the night was gone. Once her grandfather's casket was in the living room.

For a while, Julia sat and ate the cheese crackers. She told her grandmother how pretty the new burgundy wallpaper looked in the lounge. A small woman shuffled up to them with a walker and stared at the orange soda. Finally, Julia wheeled her grandmother into the living room and positioned her chair in front of the blaring television in a row of other old people. She kissed her several times.

"Be good now," Julia said, holding the bewildered old face between her hands.

"Oh I will," said her grandmother.

JULIA *sees an old boyfriend*

"La lista dei vini, per favore," Lonnie Davenport said to the waiter. "I knew you would age well, but I didn't think you would turn out like this," he said to Julia. "I've missed you, kid."

"I've missed you, Lonnie," said Julia. His kinky hair was too long. He was short but taller than she remembered. "What's it been? Nine years?" Lonnie was the other man she could have really loved if she hadn't married Michael, she thought.

"The last time I saw you was at the Kentucky Derby with your sister," said Lonnie.

"No, we saw each other in New York at Paulette Springer's wedding."

"I was pissed at you for not coming alone," he said.

"You didn't have to stay mad nine years," she said.

"You look great. You haven't gone to pot."

The waiter brought a wine list and Lonnie held up his hand to detain the man, then started asking questions in Italian about the wines.

"I didn't know you spoke Italian," she said after the waiter left.

"There are a lot of things you don't know about me."

"I'm impressed."

"I just wanted to see if the waiter really spoke it," Lonnie said. "Most of them don't."

"Remember the time we barbecued ribs and got drunk on tequila? I threw up behind the propane tank in your backyard," said Julia.

Lonnie laughed, but the laughter was gentle, in search of something else.

"The music company where I worked folded," said Julia.

"You can't trust musicians," he said.

"I want to play in a jazz club. Someday," she said.

"Here's what you do," said Lonnie. "Call Martin O'Connor's secretary tomorrow and ask her to set you up with a fellow named Bruce Stern in our office here. He handles celebrity contracts."

"Lonnie," she said, "I am not a celebrity."

"You've got to think positively," he said. He doubled both fists. "Don't let self-doubt get a foothold. What's wrong with you kid? You haven't lost your spunk, have you? You always seemed so cocksure."

"I have never felt cocksure," said Julia.

"Well don't let them know it," he said. "In the back of my mind, I always remember that somewhere I'm vulnerable and somebody could get me. But I never let them know it."

She was watching his small, delicate hands. He looked at her as if he wanted to say something else. He shook his head.

"What is it?" she said.

"I just don't believe you after nine years, Julia."

She laughed. She felt her smile taking over her face.

"Let's get out of here," he said.

"I'm not hungry either," she said.

He fixed drinks in his hotel room and they sat by the window, watching the street lamp outside. It looked like the moon.

"Make love to me," he said.

"I can't, Lonnie," she said. "I've never betrayed Michael. I don't think I ever could."

"Sure you could," he said.

"And afterward?"

"People have a right to their own fun," he said. "That is what's wrong with marriage."

"Is it why you haven't married?"

"I am married," said Lonnie. "I've been married two years." He got up and began to walk back and forth.

"Why didn't you tell me?" she said. She was stunned that Lonnie was no longer free.

"Remember we haven't talked in a long time."

"But why didn't you tell me earlier tonight?"

"Julia, I can't stand to be alone with you in this room and not touch you," he said.

She stood and without thinking moved toward him. If it was going to happen, she wanted it to happen quickly. Lonnie being married changed things. They were two adults, married to other people, in a hotel room together. The rest was inevitable. She thought about how passionate she was feeling.

"Slow down," said Lonnie. "Let's take it slow."

"I'm afraid," she said.

"So am I." He pulled her down onto the bed.

"You are?" she said. She wished she had brought a toothbrush.

"Don't cry," he said. "Everything's going to be all right." He unbuttoned her blouse.

"I'm not crying," she said. "I'm shivering."

"You're beautiful," Lonnie said, touching her breasts.

"They're small," she said.

"They're perfect," he said. He stood and pulled out his shirttail.

Julia put one arm across her breasts. Lonnie looked as if he were going to do something terrible to her. He was removing his cuff links when the phone rang.

"Let it ring," he said.

The phone rang four times then the red message button began to blink. Julia grabbed her blouse and quickly put it on. "I have to go," she said.

The corridor was empty. Julia walked quickly to the elevator. On the way down, a fat man wouldn't take his eyes off her.

"Sit in the green chair," the nurse said when they reached the small office at the end of the hall.

The nurse went out and a short doctor came in. Julia had chosen Richard Byron from the yellow pages because his name sounded tall and handsome.

"What can I do for you?" he asked.

He wore a round mirror on his forehead. Julia told him about her headache and he turned out the light. He pulled the mirror down over one eye and switched on a tiny flashlight. Julia looked at the brown eye in the hole in the center of the mirror. She thought she had a brain tumor but there was pollen in the air so she had come to an allergist.

"Are you under any stress?" Dr. Byron asked.

She said not really. "My husband has been away for a long time on business," she added.

"Why don't you go stay with him?" the doctor asked. He looked up her nose.

"I don't want to live in a motel," said Julia.

Dr. Byron shrugged. He was probably thinking she shouldn't complain if she weren't willing to go live in some motel. He told her she had a deviated septum but no signs of allergies.

"I had no idea I have a deviated septum," she said.

"It's from an old injury," he said, rotating the mirror back up onto his forehead. He turned on the light and looked at her face as if she had a skin problem.

Something had happened to her that she couldn't remember and she carried the scar, she thought.

"Depressed people get headaches," said Dr. Byron.

Julia started to cry. "I miss my husband," she said.

Once she had started crying, Julia could not stop. She felt as if her heart were being rinsed in secret, cool water. She cried in front of the receptionist as she paid the bill and in the drugstore afterward. Driving home, Julia noticed the headache was gone. Then she began to grow angry with Michael for leaving her alone.

"What do you mean you felt attracted to him?" Michael said. "It sounds like something happened."

"It was unfinished business," said Julia. "I've known Lonnie Davenport a lot longer than I've known you."

Michael hadn't even had time to unpack. Julia wasn't sure why she did it, but she had brought up Lonnie Davenport right away.

"What happened?" Michael asked. He didn't seem all that interested.

"Nothing important," she said. "What happened to you while you were gone?"

They were standing in the kitchen. "I didn't bring this up," said Michael. "I have nothing to report." He put his glass under the tap and filled it half full of water. The glass contained Scotch but he had not drunk any of it.

"You mean you refuse to tell me," said Julia. "You are the most untalkative person I have ever met. Sometimes I could scream." She shut her eyes and screamed. Her face felt split open, contorted, her teeth too big.

"Stop screaming," Michael shouted.

She pulled him around to face her and screamed in his face again with her eyes wide open. He slammed his glass down on the counter.

"Leave me alone," he said. "I just got home. I'm tired."

Julia hit him on the chest. "Talk to me. I hate being married to someone who won't talk," she said.

Michael grabbed her shoulders, his eyes tiny. He pushed her to the floor and straddled her stomach pinning her arms under his knees. He had upset the dog's water bowl.

"Get hold of yourself," he shouted in her face. He was shaking.

"I won't get hold of myself," she said. "I hate you."

Michael put his hands around her neck and pressed down on her collarbone until she thought it would snap. She watched his small, tight mouth and felt the cold water on her back and neck. Her husband was going to hit her, she thought as he raised his arm. She felt about two feet outside her body. Suddenly he stood up and looked at her hard. Then he walked out of the kitchen. Julia got up and opened the refrigerator. She stood there looking inside. She started to smile, then stopped. It was inappropriate to feel so much excitement.

JULIA *and michael*
have a joint session

"It looks like an opium den," said Michael.

"You've never seen an opium den," said Julia. "Really, he's a good therapist."

Wind chimes tinkled somewhere in the back of the house. Albert came into the room and shook hands with Michael.

"There's a dove nesting in that fir tree at the side of the house," Albert said to Julia.

She and Albert went to the window to look. He put his arm around her shoulder to turn her in the right direction. She was glad Michael would see that they had a relationship. Then Albert pointed to the pillows where they were to sit facing each other in a triangle.

"Let's all say something about why we're here," said Albert. "That usually helps clear the air."

Julia started crying. She couldn't help it.

"Okay, I'll go first," said Albert. "My idea in having you come together was to meet you, Michael, first of all, and to get a picture of how you two behave around each other."

"I'm here because Julia asked me to come," said Michael.

Julia reached for a Kleenex from the box on the floor. "I'm afraid to talk in front of Michael the way I talk to you, Albert," she said.

Albert smiled at her. "That's something to notice," he said. "How about you, Mike? Are you a little nervous?"

"The name is Michael. And sure I'm nervous," he said.

"Michael, don't be hostile," said Julia. "Albert's trying to help."

"I don't mind if he's hostile," said Albert.

"Well I do," said Julia.

"Why, Julia? Why can't Michael be hostile?"

"When he acts hostile, I get embarrassed," she said.

"But you two aren't tied together. You're two separate people. Why does his getting hostile affect you?" said Albert.

"Being married to a rude, hostile person reflects on me," she said.

Michael laughed. "This is typical. If I so much as raise an eyebrow, she gets bent out of shape and I think it's my fault."

"Have you ever considered the idea that it isn't your fault?" said Albert.

"She blames me."

"Wow," said Albert. "This is serious." He laughed.

"Why are you laughing," said Julia.

"Don't you see what you're doing?" said Albert.

"No," said Julia.

Albert did not explain it. Julia compared them, Albert in his tan pants and shirt that looked like a janitor's clothes and Michael in a dark suit, both sitting cross-legged on floor pillows.

"Someone say something," she said.

"Why?" said Albert.

"Because we're wasting money," she said.

Michael stared at her. "I've never seen you this uptight. Why are you so upset, babe?"

She started crying again.

"She's afraid you'll find out who she is," said Albert.

Julia glared at him.

"I feel terrible when you cry," Michael said in a soft voice.

For an instant Julia felt so much tenderness for him, he frightened her.

"Well this is ridiculous," she said. "I'm being silly. I'm sorry, everybody." Her voice was plucky.

"What are you doing?" said Albert.

"What am I doing?" she said, incredulous. "If I'd known you were going to be on Michael's side, he could have come by himself."

"Whoa," said Albert.

"Nobody's criticizing you," said Michael.

She stared at the two of them allied against her and clenched her fist as if it held the tender moment.

JULIA *has an erotic dream*

Julia saw herself dancing in a sheer robe, one she had never owned. It flowed around her as she whirled. Under the robe was a Chinese red nightgown with pale blue flowers. Her partner was an Oriental man with black hair to his shoulders. He wore a black kimono.

Then she was in a small room with narrow beds side by side. They had reached it by climbing a wooden ladder. Outside the room snow covered the ground. Julia let her nightgown fall around her ankles. The man undressed, too.

His skin was dry and smooth under her fingers and his hair coarse. As he kissed her stomach, she glanced at the window and saw a small corner of frost. She caressed his slender back, seeing that he was only a boy. In the moonlight his face grew wizened over hers. He grimaced but did not make a sound. Julia watched the cold stars behind his head, beyond the room, and felt nothing. The bony fingers of a thin branch tapped the window twice. She heard someone go by in the hall outside the room. Then there was a knock on the door.

Julia saw Michael's bare shoulder in the moonlight. She kissed it. His skin was warm and damp. She was relieved that she had not really made love to another man. Her life was still in order.

But now she felt everything. She felt afraid and lonely and unloved. She whispered Michael's name but he did not wake up. In the darkness of their room, she longed for the man in the kimono.

"I won't ever wear that thing," said Michael.

Julia held up the chocolate-colored kimono. "I think it would look nice on you," she said.

"Julia," said Michael. "Sit down."

She put the kimono back into the box. "It doesn't matter. I can return it. It was only an idea." The tissue rustled as she covered the garment with it.

"I'm going to be leaving the firm," said Michael.

Julia sat down in the wing chair.

"Snyder called me in this morning and said it would be best if we parted company."

"You were fired," said Julia. "That's great."

"What's so great about it?" he said.

"You took some risks and wouldn't compromise yourself. A big company isn't interested in a man who thinks for himself." She took the kimono out of the box again. "Sure you won't reconsider?"

"I thought you'd be upset."

"Do you know how depressed you've been the past eight months?" she said.

"Have I been depressed?"

"You've been very depressed," said Julia.

"In the back of my mind, I felt this coming."

"Oh Michael," she said. "I have this fantasy of us living on the water in a big frame house with screened-in porches. I see you working in the garage with a child tottering around after you. I could do some composing."

"What would I be doing in the garage?" he said, lighting a cigarette.

"I don't know. Think of something."

"I've always wanted to run a marina," he said. "I saw an ad in the paper for one with an apartment over the supply and bait shop."

"I would never live over a supply and bait shop," she said.

"You'd get used to it." He grinned.

"I would never get used to it," she said.

"What do you want me to do, Julia?" he said.

"I want you to be happy, Michael," she said. "But I don't want to give up what we already have."

"You have to make sacrifices to get what you want in life," he said. "You have to make commitments." He looked at her as if he had never seen her before.

Julia folded the kimono for the second time. "How long do you have to find another job?" she said.

"Six months. And Julia," said Michael. "I'm resigning. Don't tell people I was fired."

"What would you do if I had an affair?" Julia whispered.

"We wouldn't have time to discuss it, I'd leave you so fast," said Michael. They were in bed.

"Really?"

"Are you thinking of having an affair?" Michael put his hand on her breast.

"Sometimes I think about it." She rolled toward him.

"Really." He kissed her throat.

"Be very quiet," said Julia.

"Why?"

"Pretend you're a stranger. My husband is asleep in the next room. We have to hurry and we can't make any noise."

JULIA's *family comes to visit*

"After the war your folks had such a hard time," said Aunt Mosey. Her real name was Penelope Susan. "I took you girls an awful lot in the afternoons."

"I remember that house," said Jennifer. "Wasn't it the old one on River Street?" She set down her coffee cup.

Jennifer sounded so bright, so interested. She was full of questions. Julia thought this was because she had just returned from London.

Mosey looked out the window at the patio. "Oh, look at that cardinal so pretty in the azalea."

"He's there a lot," said Julia. She stood up to look, then sat down again at the kitchen table. It seemed sudden that Aunt Mosey was old. Her hair had turned almost white, but she insisted that it was still so blond, you could hardly see the gray.

"Why did you take care of us so much?" said Julia.

"Your mother wasn't strong there for a while," Mosey said with a frown.

"After Jen was born, I thought she didn't want me," said Julia. After Jennifer was born, Julia had tried hard to be a good girl. She tried to be perfect.

"Your mother was crazy about both you girls," Mosey said. "Harold didn't get paid much in those years, but we still had more than your folks. Yes, it was that house on River. We had a big garden in back. Every summer your mother and I canned tomatoes, beans, peas, corn, peppers. Then we'd go up to Dad's and dress chickens to freeze. I remember one day we killed fifty." She spoke with determination.

Julia had heard things over the years, but the picture was never put together this way. As far as she knew, there was nothing exceptional about her childhood. She thought her first memory might have been boredom. She never felt nostalgic for the past.

"What was Uncle Harold like?" said Jennifer. She poured herself another cup of coffee and waved the pot toward Julia. Julia said no.

"He was good through and through and a gentleman. He was quiet," Mosey said. "Harold loved children. He tried and tried to teach all you kids to draw. The only one who showed any promise was your cousin."

"Priscilla," said Julia, remembering Priscilla's hair getting so long and heavy, it started to fall out.

Mosey sipped her coffee neatly. She looked as if she were only pretending to drink. She was the one in the family most addicted to caffeine.

"Harold was very clean-minded. He never even told me a dirty joke," she said.

"Were you close?" Julia asked.

"We were," said Mosey. She had been looking at the stove. Most of the time she didn't look at the person to whom she was speaking. "He wasn't a demonstrative person, especially in public. Except once. After his first gallery show in St. Louis, he put his arm around me in front of everybody. I'll never forget it." She laughed but her eyes filled with tears. She took another dry-looking sip of coffee and set the cup down with finality. Then she rubbed her hands as if she were putting lotion on them.

"Morning," Julia's mother said, coming into the kitchen. Lillian was Mosey's younger sister. She wore a quilted bathrobe. Her hair looked as if she hadn't slept on it.

"Coffee?" Jennifer got up and opened a cupboard.

"I'll get it," Julia said, annoyed. Jennifer was always nosing around in her cupboards, her closet, her drawers.

"What a pretty day," Lillian said. "Look at that cardinal in the azalea." She touched the window.

"I think I'll go get dressed," Mosey said, standing up. "I only brought two dresses and you've seen them both."

"That doesn't bother us," Lillian said without looking at her.

"I think I'll get dressed, too," said Jennifer.

"Did you sleep all right, Mom?" Julia said after they left. It wasn't the question she wanted to ask.

"We slept like logs," her mother said.

Julia did not know what she wanted from her mother, but she felt scared. "Would you like an English muffin?" she asked.

"I'll wait until your father gets up." Her mother yawned and sang "ho hum." She sat down.

She had always seemed deliberate. She always called Julia's father "your father." All at once Julia had the feeling her mother was just killing time, and she started to cry.

"What is it, honey?" Lillian asked.

"Michael got fired," Julia said.

Her mother looked relieved. She lifted her hand, then lowered it.

Julia stopped crying. "I don't know what we're going to do," she said.

"Something will come along. It always does," her mother said.

"We had a fight this morning. I feel awful."

"I wish you kids wouldn't fight." Lillian sighed.

"Other people have fights," Julia said in a hopeful voice.

"We aren't other people," said her mother.

Julia sighed.

"Try to understand what he's going through," her mother said. "Don't argue with him. It's hard on a man's ego when he loses his job."

"What about me, Mom? I lost my job, too."

"Then you know just how he feels." Lillian folded her hands on the table.

"Don't you and Dad ever fight?"

"We disagree, but we don't fight."

"I wish you did," Julia said. "I might have learned how."

"Why fight when you can have a civil discussion?" Lillian said.

Julia remembered her mother ending discussions almost as soon as they began.

"What do you do with your anger, Mom?"

"I put it into perspective." Lillian rearranged her hands.

"Why don't you want the other person to know you're angry?"

Lillian put her hand over her heart. "Getting angry means you're losing control," she said.

Julia put an English muffin into the toaster. She waited for it to pop up. When it did, she pushed it back down. Her mother smiled at her and raised her eyebrows as if something were about to begin.

"Do you love me, Mom?" Julia asked.

"Oh honey," Lillian cried. "What have I ever done to make you think I didn't love you?"

"It isn't anything you did," said Julia. She looked at her tile floor. "I always wanted you to brush my hair," she whispered. She felt ashamed. "I don't remember you brushing our hair."

"I thought I did." Her mother's eyes were bright with tears. Her voice was breathless. She was holding her heart, still.

"Your father lost his job not long after we were married," Lillian said behind Julia. Julia sat on a kitchen chair while her mother stood brushing her hair. "I had to be strong for both of us. I gave until I thought my heart would break."

Julia had never felt so loved. She closed her eyes to save her tears. Her mother's voice washed over her.

"Then I got pregnant with you," Lillian said, "and I gave some more."

JULIA *confides in jennifer*

"Dorothy was my best friend," said Julia. "Why couldn't you make your own friends? Why did you steal mine?"

"What makes you think I wanted to steal your friends?" Jennifer asked. She poured more sherry into both their glasses. They had just come back from putting everybody on a plane. They sat on the living room floor in front of the fireplace. There was no fire.

"Think about it a minute," Julia said. "Isn't it possible that you really did try to take Dorothy away from me?"

"I liked Dorothy and Dorothy liked me," Jennifer said, stretching her legs. She had on the bathrobe Michael had given Julia. "It had nothing to do with you."

"My hair would never do right," said Julia. "You always looked prettier and you were funny. People liked you better. I think you worked at it."

"What are you trying to say?" Jennifer asked.

Julia looked at Jennifer's delicate nose. Her mouth was fuller and more appealing, but her jaw was too square. "Admit it," she said.

"Admit what?" said Jennifer.

"That you felt competitive with me."

"My God, you're analytical," said Jennifer.

"You're just like Michael," Julia said. She felt endangered. Jennifer failed increasingly to see her point of view.

"I never tried to beat you out of anything important," said Jennifer. "I didn't have to. You were always doing yourself in."

Julia looked into the cold fireplace. "I felt like shit," she said, "like I was on the verge of being crowded out of a room."

"But look at you now," said Jennifer. "You have a terrific life. I don't have the things you have."

"I think Michael would rather be married to someone else. I think he would rather be married to you."

"Julia. Michael loves you. Don't you know?"

Julia tried to smile. She despised herself for sounding desperate. She wanted to get drunk, destroy something.

"Dorothy liked you first and best," Jennifer said. "You always had closer friends than I did and I felt left out. But I wasn't trying to take her away."

"I didn't know you saw me like that," said Julia. "I never thought I had anything you might envy."

"You do. Look at your hair. How did it get darker than mine? It looks so healthy. What do you do to it? What do you eat?"

Julia could not figure out why on earth she had insisted on Jack. Michael could have found someone else. Jack sat in the wing chair with a brandy glass in one hand, talking to Michael but looking at Julia and Jennifer. He gave them equal amounts of his attention. Julia wanted more than half. She had known him first.

Michael got up and stretched. Automatically Julia got up, too. Now Jack would rise to leave, she thought. But he did not. So. He was going to stay. She nearly sat down again. Jennifer smiled at them from the sofa as if she owned it.

"Good night," said Jack. He half rose to shake Michael's hand.

Upstairs, Jennifer's toylike laugh came through the floorboards into their bedroom, which was directly over the living room. Up came the sound of shifting furniture. Why were they moving the sofa? Then ice clinked into a glass. Jennifer was making herself at home fixing more drinks. Michael tried to put his arm around Julia's stomach, the way they usually started off to sleep. She pushed him away and lay listening.

"Why are you so grumpy?" he said.

Julia closed her eyes. The conversation below was audible but not intelligible. She tried to stay awake. The next thing she heard was rhythmic sighs, or what sounded like rhythmic sighs. She sat straight up in bed. She couldn't possibly sleep with all that commotion going on beneath her. It was an outrage. Didn't they have any common courtesy? They should have gone to a motel. Julia buried her head under the pillow unwilling to listen to the end. In the suffocating darkness she saw herself at lunch with Jack two weeks earlier. She remembered in humiliating detail her foolish reticence, her giddy mood. How could she have hung onto Jack's words and his perfect smile as if they were life's very blood?

Furious, Julia got out of bed. She would go to the bathroom and make enough clatter that they would stop. As she walked down the hall, she saw a line of light under the guest room door. She tapped and Jennifer's voice told her to come in. Julia opened the door. Jennifer was in bed reading.

"I thought Jack was still here," Julia said. "I thought I might come down for a nightcap. I can't sleep."

"He's kind of boring, don't you think?" Jennifer said. She closed the book on her finger. "That smile. I didn't trust it. And the way he talks. He sounds too smooth. I couldn't wait for him to leave."

Julia closed the door and went downstairs in her bare feet. She sat on the sofa in the dark. She sat for a long time.

How do you tell someone you wish she were dead without upsetting her? Julia thought, soaping her face. She looked in the mirror and watched her fingers work the lather over her skin. A death wish was most likely a stray thought that represented something else. She could say it quickly, then laugh. She put her hands up as if she meant no harm, to see what it looked like in the mirror.

Or she could admit to Jennifer that she was ashamed of this thought. She didn't understand it herself. Could Jennifer make sense of it?

When Julia got downstairs, Jennifer had already made coffee. She sat at the kitchen table smoking and reading the paper. Julia poured a cup and sat down. She stared at Jennifer.

"Why are you staring?" said Jennifer. She put down the paper.

"I was just thinking," Julia said, "that there are times when I wish you were dead."

Jennifer was silent.

"Don't take it wrong," said Julia. "Right now I don't wish you were dead."

"Hurray," said Jennifer.

"Haven't you ever had a thought like that?"

"No I have never had a sick, perverted thought like that. Sometimes, Julia, I think you're crazy. I don't want to hear that you wish I were dead. It hurts my feelings."

"We are sisters, we have a common background, and I assumed we would have common thoughts. I guess we don't." Julia raised her chin slightly. She thought her lungs were on fire.

Michael came into the kitchen.

"Jesus Christ," he said. "Are you two at it already?"

Jennifer smiled brightly at him. Jennifer always smiled brightly at men. She acted as if it were her duty to light up the whole room, Julia thought. She considered pointing this out to Jennifer, but things were bad enough already.

"Whatever it is, I don't want to hear about it," Michael said to Julia.

So. He was on Jennifer's side.

"Michael, did you get hold of that friend of yours with the boat?" Jennifer asked. "Are we going sailing this weekend?"

As soon as Michael left, Jennifer went upstairs and started packing. Julia watched from the doorway.

"I'll go stay in a hotel. Do you know a cheap one? I don't have much money," said Jennifer.

"Don't go," Julia said.

"I don't want to stay anywhere I'm not wanted."

"It isn't that I wish you would die, Jen," said Julia. "I thought that if I said it, you might say you'd had the same thought. And then we could talk about it."

"It's clear you hate me and I will not stay another day in a house where I am hated," said Jennifer. Her face looked ready to break into a scream.

Julia put the side of her right fist on B-flat and C-sharp. Jolly straightened her wrist and positioned her elbow. He had accepted her as a student the month before.

"Drop your elbow and let the weight play the notes," he said. "Relax." He made her do it ten times.

Julia felt murderous. She thought of Jennifer in the cockpit of Fred's boat, a look of innocence and joy on her face that any man would appreciate. Julia couldn't stand that look. She couldn't stand her sister.

"That's better," Jolly said. "What else have you been working on?"

She didn't feel up to it but she turned to the ballad she had practiced all week. She didn't care how it sounded. She improvised four choruses. Each time she came to the break, Julia felt so lonely inside, such loneliness around her in the room, she almost cried. She thought of Jennifer and felt sorry. When she had finished, she sat looking at her hands. They looked like an older woman's hands.

"That's the best you've ever played for me, Julia," said Jolly. He touched her back. "Are you all right?"

She said nothing. It was the first time he had ever said her name to her.

"Is something wrong?" he asked.

"I've been attracted to you for some time," she said. She could not believe she had said it. It was not even relevant. She felt angry again.

Jolly was quiet. He looked at her as if he were trying to make up his mind about something. Was he going to confess he had been holding himself back waiting for some sign from her? He took his hand from her back.

"I shouldn't have said that," she said. "It's been a bad week."

"I'm hip," he said. He raised his hand but did not finish the gesture. He looked at her hard. He was a man she would never know. She envied the woman who would.

JULIA *goes to the gynecologist*

Julia looked at the chimpanzee grinning down at her from the ceiling. The poster was captioned IS IT FRIDAY YET?

"These are your ovaries and this is your uterus," said the doctor.

"Oh," she said as he pushed down on her abdomen. "I just realized I'm looking at a chimpanzee."

"A little something to distract you," the nurse said in a bright voice.

Julia resented the voice and the chimpanzee. She closed her eyes. Before the doctor came in, she had sat shivering under the paper vest with the paper blanket over her lap, watching a tiny worm crawl along the examination table. It was most likely a pre-insect worm, something you would find on a bush, she thought. Yet the longer she looked at it, only a fraction of an inch long and slimy, the more it looked like a worm you would find in a person.

"You can sit up now," said the doctor. He did not give her a hand.

The nurse left the room, taking slides, a tiny specimen bottle, and the speculum in a paper towel. The doctor peeled off his disposable gloves and wrote something on Julia's record. She sat up.

"Anything I need to know?" he said. "Any questions?" He was a nice man. He had a stubble because he had been up all night delivering a baby.

"I'm thinking about getting pregnant," said Julia. She noticed how positive this sounded.

"Wonderful," he said. "That's what we like to hear."

"I've been reading about older women getting pregnant," she said. "I guess it's harder for them to conceive because sometimes they don't ovulate." She did not feel that she was talking about herself.

"Are your periods regular?" said the doctor. He leaned against a small metal cabinet on rollers.

She said yes and he said she must be ovulating regularly and not to worry. Then he told her what she already knew about the menstrual cycle and conception. The way he said it, the consequences did not sound grave.

"Have you ever tried to get pregnant?" he asked.

Julia had her arms folded over the paper vest to keep it shut. She thought of the worm. She said no.

"Don't worry about it unless you run into a problem," he said, "and don't believe everything you read."

"We haven't really decided yet," she said.

"It's decision-making time," he said. "You might even decide not to have a family."

Julia said nothing. She knew she would never be able to decide not to have children.

"Michael," she said. "Let's have a baby."

Michael had just turned out the light. They were in bed.

"I've had a bad day," he said.

"But you're always telling me you want a family."

"Why the rush?"

"I'm thirty-six now," said Julia.

"You told me we had another four or five years," he said.

"I'm afraid I'll change my mind."

"You've changed it a hundred times already. You'll come back around."

"But you accused me of depriving you of your right to be a father. You threatened to divorce me," said Julia. "Don't you want a baby anymore, Michael?"

"Look Julia. I'm trying to find a job," Michael said.

"I made a consultation appointment for us with my gynecologist," said Julia.

"Why do we need to consult anyone?"

"At my age the hormones could go crazy or something. There are things we should find out."

"I don't have anything to say to the man." Michael turned over with his back to her.

"Don't you have any technical questions?" she said.

"No, I think I know what I'm supposed to do," he said turning onto his stomach.

"I thought a consultation might perk up your interest and get you thinking about it again."

"I do think about it," said Michael.

"What do you think?" said Julia.

"That it might be nice to have a little girl."

"What about playing baseball with your son?"

"A boy would be okay. But I think I want a girl."

"I'm afraid she would be like me and I would be like my mother. We'd both be miserable."

"No you wouldn't," said Michael. He turned onto his back.

"I'm getting older just lying here, Michael," she said.

"So am I."

"Don't you think we ought to do something about it?"

"I have to get up at six-thirty."

"Sexual energy isn't supposed to have anything to do with physical fatigue," she said. "Albert says we're afraid to get emotionally close."

"Fuck Albert. He doesn't work as hard as I do."

Julia looked into the dark. The sheets were cool.

"Why don't you lust after me?" she said.

Michael sat up in bed.

"What is it?" she said.

"I've got a lot on my mind," he said. "I don't have time for this right now."

"I want you to think about sex more," she said. "I think you're hungry, but you're scared."

Michael reached over and grabbed her arm. "Don't analyze me," he said. "It's one thing I don't need." His voice was frightening in the dark. He pushed her arm away.

Julia listened to the room for a while, then she turned over and pretended to sleep. She held herself as if she were holding someone else.

JULIA *visits jennifer in cairo*

The air was full of sand. Children clung like insects to the backs of smoking buses. Julia watched a donkey plod through a busy intersection. The boy on its back beat its neck with a stick. The smell of urine was so rancid she started to cross the street. A man in a long violet robe drew her back by her elbow. She looked into his dark face. Was he going to try to sell her perfume? A taxi swerved inches from them. The man had saved her life. She wanted to thank him but she did not know the words in his language. She watched him disappear into the crowd.

"This scarab is almost four thousand years old, very beautiful green jasper," said the old man who owned the jewelry shop. He wore a gray suit and a lavender tie. He unlocked the case and brought the ring out for Julia. She slipped it on her finger.

"It's beautiful," she said.

"It is the heart scarab, carved to ensure eternal beating of the heart. It will bring you long life," he said.

The light from the display case reflected in his glasses. Death seemed nowhere near.

"You like our country?" he said.

"Enormously," said Julia.

"When I was a young man, I studied in Italy. I was away from home many months."

"What did you study?" Julia asked.

"Opera," he said. "I wanted to sing."

"Why didn't you stay?" said Julia. She took off the ring.

"There was the family business and it was necessary to come home," he said, shrugging as if the answer were simple.

"Did you fall in love with any Italian women?" she said, slipping the ring back on. She decided to buy it.

"I was handsome as a young man," he said.

"You're still handsome," she said. She fingered the gold chain around her neck. "I'm sorry you had to stop singing."

"I probably would never have been great, but I will always love opera. I can still sing."

The shop owner began to sing an aria in Italian. It was the strangest thing that had ever happened to her. Did he sing for all his customers? His voice made her uneasy. Unsure at first, it grew bolder. The sound was exquisite and sad. Julia knew she was making mistakes. But she did not know any other way to live. When he finished singing, the man covered his heart with both hands. What was she going to lose?

"You have a beautiful voice," she said.

He pulled a handkerchief from his pocket and wiped his eyes. "It is a beautiful song," he said.

The bazaar was quiet as Julia wound her way back through the alleys. Most of the shops were closed. On the street evening had fallen. She watched a man on the corner, one hand cupped behind his ear and the other over his mouth. He was singing his prayers. Two steps behind him his veiled wife waited. His prayers sounded lonely and inevitable. All at once, he finished and the woman followed him away.

"Why should Jim matter to you?" Jennifer said. "He's a stranger and you're married." They were sitting on Jennifer's balcony drinking tea.

"I don't feel married," said Julia. "In this country I don't even feel like myself."

Julia looked at the rooftop of the next building where a family lived in a corrugated iron shack. Two sheep wandered over the roof. In the distance a giant beer bottle rose, cut out against the sky. Stella beer. Julia listened to the honking from the street below. In the Hilton discotheque the music seemed to come from inside her head and the room broke continually into a thousand pieces of light. She had never felt so much in love.

"We're shooting at the pyramids today if you want to come watch," said Jennifer.

"I'm going out with Jim," said Julia.

Jennifer shrugged. "Do what you want," she said.

"It isn't your marriage," Julia said.

"If you only knew how much it hurts the other person." Jennifer looked at the Stella billboard.

"You don't understand why I need to do it," said Julia.

"You don't need to do it," said Jennifer. "Michael is a wonderful man." She stood and went inside.

It was too late. Julia had already done it. She felt she would never be the same again. She felt like a divided woman.

"Will you tell your wife?" she said.

Jim sat on the bed and she stood between his knees.

"She doesn't want to know," he said, unbuttoning Julia's blouse.

"I couldn't tell Michael," she said.

"Believe me. He doesn't want to know either," said Jim. He was a small man, shorter than Michael, and slighter. He had dark hair. "Never tell them is my recommendation. And don't use it to hurt them." He drew Julia's belt out of the loops and unfastened her skirt.

"Have you had many affairs?" said Julia.

"You're the fourth," he said. "I only do it out of town. Hey. Let's not talk about that."

She had hoped he would say she was special. "You're my first," she said and ran her fingers through his hair. It was wiry.

Jim stroked her arm. "I hope you want me as much as I want you," he said. "That's all I ask."

"I do," she said. He had said the same words the first time and she had responded the same.

"You look just as I dreamed you would," Jim said, stretching out on the bed. "I've undressed you a hundred times."

Julia lay beside him and ran her fingertips over his shoulder as if it were carved of ivory. She wished Michael would look at her this way. Jim pulled her against him and sighed loudly.

"What's wrong?" she whispered.

"I want you so much," he said.

Julia looked at his collarbone and the hollow above it. The world seemed very small. She looked at the lamp beside the bed and tried to put Michael out of her mind.

"Hey. Let's run away together," said Jim. "Let's go to Greece."

"Michael is expecting me on Saturday," said Julia. It was Thursday. "I have to go home."

"I'll pay for everything."

"It isn't that," said Julia.

"I'm only kidding." He rubbed her back. "Do it for us," he said.

Julia saw Michael's face searching the crowd of arriving passengers for her.

"Come on," said Jim. He held her.

Julia heard herself say all right, she would do it. She listened to her dangerous, unworried laugh.

"Hello spontaneity," said Jim.

JULIA *runs away with jim*

Walking toward her through the Athens airport, Jim seemed shorter, thinner, and looked fretful. She knew he had gone to the duty-free shop to buy presents for his wife and children. It was Saturday morning. An amplified voice announced a flight delay.

"Sweetie," said Jim.

She couldn't stand being called "sweetie."

"You look tired. Do you want to get a drink?" he said.

"It is eleven in the morning," said Julia. She was thinking of the flight to New York at one.

"Let's see about a car then," said Jim. They had planned to spend four days driving through the Greek countryside. He looked at her, his eyes full of misery and need. It was the look she had taken for desire.

"I want to go home," she said.

The corridor behind Jim seemed endless and it was littered. A noisy family rushed by dragging luggage on rollers. Jim put his free arm around her shoulder.

"I don't know what it is about getting on a plane and leaving," Julia said remembering the look on Jennifer's face when they left Cairo.

"I know," said Jim. "You've got the jitters. Let's have a drink and talk about it."

As she drank, Julia felt herself rise out of the flatness of the morning. Jim began to look better to her against the background of low purple furniture and foil wallpaper in the bar. Humility and desire returned to his eyes.

"Let's skip Greece and go to Paris," said Jim. He put his hands over both of hers as if he were trying to prevent her from doing something destructive.

"I don't have enough money," she said.

"I do," he said.

The curtain had peacocks on it. Julia pushed the peacocks aside and looked down into the narrow street. A gray Le Car identical to the one she and Michael had rented was parked half on the sidewalk below. She knew Michael wasn't going to walk in but it seemed a possibility. She had sent him a telegram saying her plane was rerouted through Paris. Jim was sitting on the bed, trying to uncork a bottle of champagne. With their luggage opened on the floor, they could hardly walk around the bed, the room was so small. She heard the cork pop and turned around.

"What shall we do tonight," she said. "I know. There's a darling restaurant over by the Sorbonne."

"Let's make a reservation," said Jim.

Julia stepped over her suitcase and reached for the phone. Jim caught her arm and put a water glass full of champagne into her hand. "Here's to Paris," he said. "Here's to us."

She loved it when he did things like that.

"Remember the Casino des Pigeons?" said Jim.

"We had fun in Cairo," she said.

"And we'll have fun in Paris," he said.

"*Gracias*," Jim said to the waiter.

"It's *merci*," Julia said, laughing to show she wasn't being critical. She took the menu from the waiter who then whisked her napkin off the table and drew it across her lap. They sat at a small table in a room with a low ceiling and old stone walls. Julia liked the circle of light around the candle and the darkness beyond that. She liked being able to see only part of Jim.

A gray-haired couple sat at the table in the corner. Julia envied them. They were handsome people and well dressed. When they spoke, they looked directly into each other's eyes. She should not have brought him here, she thought. This place belonged to her and Michael.

"*Madame?*" said the waiter.

Julia looked at Jim and said she wasn't ready to order.

"I can't stay here," she said when the waiter had gone.

"Are you sick?" he said. He drove his eyebrows together.

Julia started to laugh. "I'm sorry," she said, stopping. "You look so worried."

"What is it, dear?" he said.

Being called "dear" made her irritable.

"Please, let's just leave," she said.

As she walked away from the table, she heard Jim explain to the waiter that she had gotten ill. He spoke carefully, as if he were talking to an old person, even though the waiter was fluent in English. She thought he probably treated his children the same way, never letting them touch his heart.

At the hotel Julia waited in the small lobby while Jim went up to call his wife. She sat in a chair upholstered in luxurious burgundy brocade. Beside her was a fresh arrangement of mixed flowers in a brass pot. The night clerk, a slender, attractive young man in a crewneck sweater, was reading a poem to an older man who sat by his desk in a straight-backed chair. The man listened, nodding in rhythm, both hands resting on the knob of the cane that stood between his knees. He had a neat mustache and wore a red ascot.

"Julia." Jim's voice came from the stairs.

She ignored him. The night clerk leaned with an earnest look toward the man and spoke in rapid French. Julia understood part of it, something about the moon and the sea, or was it someone's mother? When he finished, he dropped his head for a moment, then raised it and began talking about the poem. Julia stood up, realizing that he had written it. As she crossed the lobby she watched the older man. His eyes seemed held by something in the night clerk's eyes. For a moment the man's mouth turned down as if preparing for tears. He wet his lips.

"Tomorrow is Nadia's eleventh birthday," Jim said. "I pretended I hadn't forgotten." He looked miserable.

JULIA *meets frank*

"*Madame?*" said the waiter. He looked across the street.

"*Un café au lait et un croissant avec du beurre, s'il vous plaît,*" said Julia. She inhaled the smell of a Gauloise. The man beside her opened his newspaper and folded it inside out. He wore a taupe-colored tweed jacket. He had brown hair with a lot of gray in it. His hands were small and looked as if they should belong to someone else.

"May I borrow your ashtray?" he said. He was an American.

"Certainly," Julia said, sliding it toward him. "I don't smoke."

"Good for you," he said. He put the newspaper on his table and tapped his ashes into the ashtray on her table. The tables were crowded together on the sidewalk.

"Sometimes when I smell a Gauloise, I wish I did," she said.

"No, you don't," he said. "It's a nasty habit. Say, may I join you?"

She was surprised at his height when he stood.

"Bring my coffee to this table," he said as the waiter walked by. "I'm Frank Allen," he said to Julia.

Julia told him her name. "Are you an athlete by any chance?" she said.

He laughed. "In high school I played basketball," he said, looking beyond her.

"What do you do now?" she said.

"I play the piano," he said.

"So do I," she said, looking at his hands again. Did he have trouble with his reach?

"Where do you play?" he said.

"I didn't mean I'm a professional," she said. "I'm still a student."

"I've been playing here for the last six months," he said, "but I have to go back to New York in a few weeks."

"Oh," said Julia. "Where is your gig?"

He told her the name of the club. She had never heard of it. She had never heard of him but she was impressed.

"You must play jazz, then," she said.

"And a lot of other stuff, too," he said. "You know how it is."

"I try to avoid weddings and bar mitzvahs myself," she said.

"What I mean is," he said, "Americans always want to hear 'New York, New York' or 'I Left My Heart in San Francisco.' Where do you study?"

She told him.

"I've heard of Jolly Brown. So you're working with Jolly." He looked interested.

Julia said it was a small world. That Frank knew Jolly made her feel closer to Frank.

"I was going to the Rodin Museum if you'd like to come along," he said. "Are you alone?"

"Today I am," she said. "My friend has the turistas and stayed at the hotel."

"Is your friend a man or a woman?" said Frank. He put out his cigarette.

"A woman," said Julia. She didn't know why she said it. She meant to be truthful, but when she opened her mouth, a lie came out. She laughed.

"What's funny?" Frank smiled at her. His eyes moved over her face.

"You never know what is going to happen," she said. "I'd love to hear you play."

"We can drop by the club later on," he said. "I'd like to hear you play, too."

"I'm not that good," she said.

"If you're working with Jolly, you can't be all that bad."

"I would like to go to the museum with you," she said, "and stop by your club later on." She hoped he would ask her to dinner.

"Have dinner with me, too," he said.

"Okay," she said.

"I thought I was going to be alone again today," he said. He glanced at her. "What's wrong?"

"I hope I'm more than a mere convenience," she said. She was thinking of the Tunisian dentist.

"Don't worry. You're more than a convenience," he said.

Inside the club was cold. Frank took her hand and led her through the tables to the stage, one step up. Finally she could see. The walls of the room made it look like a cave. The air was stale with cigarette smoke. Frank played exactly as she would have chosen to have him play, and he didn't look at her, which she liked. He looked across the room. Sometimes he bowed his head. If he would love her, she thought, she would feel complete. He finished with an extravagant cadenza.

"Your turn," he said standing up.

"Sit beside me," she said. "I'm not that good."

"Don't apologize."

"I just want you to know."

Julia began a Cole Porter song. It felt good. The ideas were coming. When she finished, she sat and looked at the keys, waiting for Frank to say something.

"What was that you did during the second break?" Frank played a few notes.

Julia couldn't remember what she had done.

"I thought maybe you were just talking," he said, "but you really can play."

"You said I couldn't be all that bad."

"I know. I was just being nice."

"Don't just be nice," she said, finding his eyes in the dim light.

Frank kissed her mouth. She knew her lips felt as soft as his. A door opened at the end of the bar.

"*C'est moi*," Frank said.

"*C'est vous?* Okay." The door shut.

"Julia, let me take you to my place," said Frank.

They walked up three flights of old wooden stairs.

"This apartment is modest by Parisian standards. By American, it's the pits," he said.

"It doesn't matter," she said. She watched his back move.

He lit a match and put the key in the keyhole. Then he turned around and kissed her. "Here we go," he said, opening the door.

The room was furnished with torn, shabby furniture. The curtains were sheets.

"Don't put tissue down the stool," he said. "The plumbing isn't any good. I have to turn the water off every time I go out. Here's the kitchen." He pushed back a folding partition. Behind it were a sink, two burners, and a small refrigerator. He twisted a knob under the sink. "The water's back on," he said.

Julia looked out the window at the gray brick of the neighboring building.

"Can I get you some whiskey?" said Frank. He crossed the room and touched her hair.

"This place is another world," she said. If it had been at all familiar, she would have wondered what she was doing there.

Frank led her up the narrow staircase to the loft. On the floor was a double mattress covered with a nylon sleeping bag that had been unzipped and spread out like a blanket.

"It's funny," Frank said as he took off his jacket. He hung it up in the small closet. "When I was a kid, I imagined living in a place like this. It didn't have to be nice, just private."

"Did you have a lot of brothers and sisters?" Julia said. Frank helped her pull her turtleneck over her head.

"No. I think it was more that I didn't have myself. I was a model kid. My parents' friends liked me better than they liked their own kids. This place gets cold at night, though. Sometimes the heat doesn't work."

"You poor thing," said Julia.

"You're a lovely woman," said Frank. His voice was melodious and the way he spoke made her feel irresistible.

He took off his shirt. Underneath, he wore a bright yellow T-shirt with RUGBY printed on it. Julia laughed.

"I didn't get to the laundry," he said trying to find the hooks on the back of her bra.

"It unhooks in front," she said. She let the straps fall over her shoulders and down her arms.

"How about you?" he said, moving his lips against her ear. "Did you have brothers and sisters? Did you have a self?"

"I have a sister," said Julia. "We used to be close. But recently, I began to realize how different we are."

"My poor darling," he said in her hair. He unzipped his pants and took them off. He was not wearing any underwear. "I became an athlete to prove I wasn't weird," he said. "It's funny how you fight yourself when you're a kid."

Julia kissed his chest. She thought he understood her. "My first improvisation teacher was gay," she said. "My mother made me quit when she found out."

"In high school I started a band. We played for grown-up dances."

"I can't believe this," said Julia. "I can't believe I found you. I've known you for at least two hundred years." She unfastened her skirt and slipped it off. Then she folded her clothes and put them on top of a cardboard box full of paperbacks.

"Are you going to tell me what you're really doing in Paris?" he said.

"I was afraid you would go away if I told you," she said. He did understand her.

"I might have," he said. He touched the tip of her nose with one finger. "You were pretty smart."

"My friend is a man named Jim," she said.

"So old Jim has the turistas."

"There's more," she said. "My husband's name is Michael."

Frank said nothing.

"For months I wanted to have an affair. I went to two shrinks because I thought there was something wrong with me. Have you ever been married?"

"I'm getting divorced," he said.

"Any kids?" she said. She pulled off her panty hose.

"A little girl," he whispered. "I miss her."

"I can imagine," said Julia. Children complicated things, she thought.

Frank pushed down her panties. He touched her.

"I came to Paris to try and get my head together," he said. "It's been lonely." He pulled her toward the bed.

"Maybe I should have gotten lonely," said Julia, "but I couldn't stand it." They got into bed. Julia looked at the ceiling. "The toilet is running," she said.

"I know," he said. "Would you like to smoke some dope?"

"Drugs make me paranoid," she said.

"We won't do much," he said. He got up and went to the chest of drawers. He pulled out a top drawer. His shoulders were not as broad as they appeared when he had on his jacket.

"I need something to slow me down," said Frank. He lit the pipe, sucked on it three times, and knelt on the mattress to hand it to Julia. "You really arouse me," he said.

The way he looked at her, she felt he was entering her through her eyes. He was entering her world, she thought. She drew on the pipe and held the smoke in her lungs. Finally she had to cough.

"Don't take so much next time," he said. He got back in bed. "I wonder if we'll get too hot under this bag."

Julia looked at his face just as he looked at the ceiling.

"I wonder what's going to happen," he said.

Someone knocked, then pounded on the door downstairs. A woman's voice shouted Frank's name.

"Shit," he said. He got out of bed, put on his robe, and went down.

Julia listened intently. Frank spoke in French to the woman. Julia hadn't known he could speak French so well. Then the door shut and she heard him come back up the stairs.

"Damn it," he said. "Don't let that bother you."

What kind of a man had women pounding on his door in the middle of the day?

"Where were we?" he said.

"I'd better call the hotel," she said.

"The phone doesn't always work," said Frank. He handed her his robe.

It took her a while to get the number of the hotel. She stared out at the gray brick wall and waited for the desk clerk to answer. The texture of the brick made her think of Russia.

"I missed you," Jim's voice said. "At least when I was awake I missed you. But I'm glad you found someone to pal around with. Where is she from?"

"Are you feeling better?" Julia said.

"Julia," he said, "I made a reservation to fly home tomorrow. I've got to get back."

"I understand," she said.

"Will I see you tonight?"

"I don't think so," she said. She was examining a single brick now.

"Are you staying on?" he said.

"I think so," she said.

Neither of them spoke.

"So you aren't coming back tonight," he finally said.

"Not unless you think I should."

"I'm not going to tell you what to do, dear," he said. "Julia, you sound funny."

She wanted to say that knowing him had meant something, but it seemed too much to put into words.

"Have a nice life, Julia," Jim said.

She hung up. "This is ridiculous," she said.

"What?" Frank said upstairs.

She went up and took off the robe.

"Everything all right?" he said as she slid back in beside him.

She pressed herself against him. His voice sounded far away. She could not tell what was happening to her.

JULIA *returns*

"What were you doing in Paris?" said Michael. He put his arm around her shoulders, but roughly.

"Michael, I just got back," Julia said, laughing. "Welcome me home."

"I want an explanation," said Michael.

"I told you in the telegram. My flight went through Paris and I arranged to stay a couple of days for the same fare."

"You stayed a week," said Michael.

They were walking through the airport. It was Saturday afternoon. Julia saw only the squares of gray linoleum moving past her feet. She had kissed his thighs. He had put his cock in her mouth. She closed her eyes. "Really, Michael. All it cost was a little for the hotel."

"Money isn't what worries me," said Michael.

Julia looked at the fat man rushing toward them. He was loaded down with bags. He wore two cameras around his neck.

"It has nothing to do with you," she said. "Stop being so hard on me. You look so hard." They each carried one of her bags.

"Irene said she'd give us a free pitcher when you got back," said Michael.

"Irene?"

"At McGraw's. God, Julia."

"Oh. Irene," she said. She touched the bracelet Frank had given her. He wouldn't be back in the States for three weeks.

"Several people asked me where you were," said Michael.

"I'm surprised," she said.

"Surprised at what?" he said.

"That I was missed by your friends," she said.

"They're your friends, too," he said.

At McGraw's Irene gave them a free pitcher. "There it is," she said, setting it down.

Julia smiled at her, but Irene did not smile back. She went away.

"It's hard to believe that woman cares about anyone," said Julia.

"She cares. We had a long talk one night."

Julia looked over at Irene propped against the bar watching television. Michael poured the beer.

"I did a lot of thinking while you were gone," he said. He took a drink. "I want us to have a good marriage, Julia. I want to have kids and love each other and be close."

Julia looked at him. "What makes you say that now?"

"I was all ready to have you come home when I got this telegram saying my wife is staying in Paris," he said as if he were bragging. "I was furious." He grinned.

"That's funny," said Julia. She felt that less of her was sitting there in the booth than had been moments before. She looked at Irene again. A man sat at the bar now. The back of his head looked like Frank's. Julia knew it could not be Frank. Finally he turned and she saw his profile. His nose was too big, his mouth was all wrong, and he wasn't even nice looking.

"Cissy asked me what was wrong with you," said Michael. "You didn't say two words all evening." He poured himself a cup of coffee.

"I didn't have two words to add," Julia said putting on water for poached eggs, "to an evening-long conversation on writs, habeas corpuses, and quonum borums."

"What's the matter with you?" he said.

"There must be something the matter with me if Cissy Miller says there is," said Julia.

"She was concerned," said Michael.

"Then why aren't you?" said Julia. "All you seem to care about is whether or not I offended your fraternity brother's wife."

"My fraternity brother's wife. People aren't people to you, are they? They're positions."

"Cissy's at ten o'clock."

"What?" said Michael. He sat down at the table.

"I see her in the upper left-hand corner of my life."

"I don't know what you're talking about."

"You're at six o'clock." Julia stared at the exhaust fan over the stove. "Aren't I at noon for you?"

"I don't understand you anymore," said Michael. "You're miles away. You never want to do anything. You don't like anybody." He opened his newspaper.

"Look how short I keep my nails, Michael." She showed him her nails. "That's because I'm a pianist."

"I know. I hear you practicing at six in the morning."

"I thought you couldn't hear me over the humidifier," she said.

"You play the piano all the time," he said. "You never want to leave the house. The house is a mess. When is the last time you washed our sheets? When did you vacuum the rug?"

Calmly, Julia cracked an egg and dropped it into the boiling water. Then she cracked another egg.

JULIA *goes looking for antiques*

"I'm taking inventory today," said the woman. Her hair was dyed the color of a pumpkin and she had no eyebrows. She could have been forty or she could have been sixty. "Then I'll know how much has been stolen." She stood behind the screen door of the small frame house. "Tillie's Antiques" was painted on a plank of wood over the door.

"Are you open?" Julia said. She stepped up onto the porch, which was overrun by used furniture.

"If there's just the one of you, I guess I could let you in." She took her hands out of the large pockets of her house dress and unhooked the screen door.

Several chamber pots sat in a row at the foot of the stairs. On the wall was a set of moose antlers with a man's jacket hanging on it. "Are you Tillie?" said Julia.

"No," she said. "Tillie's dead. I'm Mildred."

"Nice to meet you, Mildred," said Julia. She followed Mildred into the dim front room. The air smelled musty.

"Tillie was my sister."

"I'm sorry," Julia said.

"It was a blessing when the Lord took her home."

"That's some consolation," Julia said. She looked around at the shelves of glassware. "Do you have any cut glass?" she said.

"You'll have to speak up," said Mildred. She went behind a display case. "Lots of my best pieces, small pocket-size pieces, has been taken." She unfastened a safety pin from the front of her dress and removed a key that she used to unlock the china cupboard. "They come right up on the porch and take things. I put broken stuff on the porch." She handed Julia two goblets.

Frank could have this room, Julia thought. A grand piano would go in the corner by the window. She would fill the window with plants, and she was thinking of a hunter green wallpaper with ducks on it that she had seen.

"These look like pressed glass," Julia said.

"Not many women my age could run this shop," Mildred said. "I bet you can't guess how old I am."

"I'd say you're not over sixty," said Julia.

"I'm seventy-three," said Mildred. She smiled.

"You certainly don't look it," Julia said.

"Now them's English," Mildred said, pointing to the goblets. "Last week I had a set of sherry glasses somebody stole that I could of showed you." She locked the goblets back inside the cupboard.

"I can't believe people come in here and steal things," Julia said.

"Oh they do. I got some globe lamps just in from an estate sale if that interests you. You know the Walkers?"

"I don't believe I do," said Julia. She followed Mildred into the next room.

This room would be hers. Light fell through the branches of a tree just outside the window and made a pattern on the wall. The pattern shimmered and moved. Julia looked at a shelf of china dolls' heads. The white faces stared out at nothing.

"You can stay for tea," said the woman. She walked out of the room.

"I think I'd better get going," Julia called after her.

"Now the English have marmalade with their tea." The voice came from the back of the house. Julia followed the sound into the kitchen.

Mildred took a jar of orange marmalade out of the refrigerator and put a kettle of water on the gas stove. Julia sat at the small formica table. On the counter was a cookie jar in the shape of a priest in a brown robe with THOU SHALT NOT STEAL painted across his fat belly. Julia watched Mildred unknot a bag of Wonder Bread and put two slices in the oven. She listened to the hiss of gas.

"Did you ever dream something and think it was real?" Mildred opened the oven and looked at the bread. "I dreamed Howard came home last night. Howard was my companion for nineteen years."

Julia had seen Frank's face so clearly in the night, she thought he was in the room. When she woke up, she couldn't remember what he looked like.

"In dreams, no time passes," said Mildred. She put the bread on two saucers. "I miss Howard." She set the saucers on the table.

"You aren't thinking of moving out of this house, by any chance?" Julia asked. With Frank time seemed not to pass.

"One of these days," said Mildred, "my nephew's coming to get me."

"When do you think that might be?" Julia glanced around the kitchen. Why couldn't she remember his face?

"He lives in Alabama."

"Could you remember to call me when he comes?" Julia said.

"Maybe I could," said the woman. She looked at the calendar on the wall by the stove. The calendar was ten years old.

Julia took a laundry claim check out of her purse.

"I'll write down my name and number on this," she said.

She got out a ballpoint pen. The claim check was for Michael's shirts. She turned it over. On the back she wrote her maiden name and seven numbers.

JULIA *takes the train to new york*

Julia put her bag in the luggage rack overhead and sat in the seat by the window. A man paused and looked at her, then went on. She stared out the window. The train jerked and started to move. As it picked up speed, it seemed to flow out of the covered station into the bright sunshine. She listened to the clack of the wheels underfoot. The slums went by and then an industrial park. Finally they were in the country. She felt that she was nowhere, that she could not be seen.

When they were seventeen, she and Jennifer took the train to Chicago. They wandered through the cars, ending up in the baggage compartment with an old conductor. He told them to sit on a trunk and shoved the door wide open so they could see out. The three of them watched the countryside go by like a silent movie. The conductor sucked on a toothpick and glanced at them sideways. Julia said they had to go. The conductor said not to rush off. They left before something bad could happen and smoked a cigarette in the washroom.

Ahead, three men stood talking so animatedly outside a Chinese restaurant, they looked like pantomimists. As Julia walked past, one of them caught her arm. She let herself be whirled around because she was in New York. The sunshine was cold.

"If you had a chance to go to the best Chinese restaurant in New York, what would you do?" the man asked. He put his arm around her waist. Julia recognized him but could not remember his name. He had little dark eyes close together and a busy mouth. His nose, though not as big as she remembered, made his mouth look small. He was a celebrity.

"If I were hungry," she said, "I would go into the restaurant." Julia looked at the other two men.

"Here is a young woman with good sense. What is your name, young woman?"

The celebrity linked arms with her.

"Before you, Julia, you see two hungry men outside the best Chinese restaurant in New York," he said.

"I think they should go in," she said. Was she helping him get rid of these guys?

"Okay, you two. Have a good time. See you later."

"*Bon appétit,*" said Julia.

She moved away with him, her arm clamped under his.

"I can't quite remember your name," she said. He had such heavy eyebrows, she thought she might have made a mistake. They were walking fast.

He told her his name. He was a famous comedian.

"I'm sorry," said Julia. She looked at the sidewalk not wanting to see if people were staring at them. Then she looked at the blue sky between buildings.

"Where are you going?" he asked without turning to her.

"Bloomingdale's," said Julia. She regretted having a trivial destination. They walked exactly in stride, their sides pressed together. Her legs felt long.

"I'm going to catch a boat," he said.

"A boat?"

"A boat to the island where I live." A car screeched and honked.

"You live on an island," she said.

"I have a house on an island where I stay when I come to New York," he said.

"Oh," said Julia.

"I was roasted last night." They stopped for a wait signal.

"Roasted?" She turned to him.

"Man of the year," he said and told her the name of the organization.

She had never heard of it. They stepped off the curb.

"What do you do?" he asked, looking closely at her.

"I'm a musician," she said.

"I composed a song once," he said. "For the fiftieth anniversary of the parents of a dear friend."

He began to recite the lyrics. She imagined him writing them, a pencil to his chin in the glow of a fire on a winter evening. She saw him bending over to sing it to two old people hard of hearing. Although Julia had never cared one way or another about him as a comedian, she saw now that he was a sensitive human being. She leaned her head toward him until it almost touched his shoulder. He spoke sometimes to her, sometimes to the crowded sidewalk of Fifty-ninth Street. When he had finished, she pressed her lips tightly together and gave him an earnest look. She wondered if he would ask her to come out to his island.

"Say, if you want advice about getting into the entertainment business," he said, "you can call my lawyer."

Julia thought he was going to say she could call him. Bloomingdale's lay just ahead.

"Your lawyer doesn't want to hear from me," she said.

The comedian insisted that his lawyer would be glad to help her and made her repeat the name and phone number.

"I have a friend who might need some help," she said.

They walked to the Lexington Street entrance of Bloomingdale's.

Julia would tell the comedian that she was meeting her friend at one o'clock. She would love to see the island but there wasn't time. She thought his house would be modern and cool inside with large glass windows looking out on water that glittered in the moonlight.

He wished her luck, repeated his lawyer's name, and kissed her hand. He had asked her to remove her glove first. Then he walked briskly away and crossed Lexington before the light changed. With the celebrity gone, Julia felt as if someone had just taken back the beautiful fur coat she was wearing.

Frank stood with his hands in the pockets of his windbreaker. His face had no color and no expression. He seemed to have lost weight. Across the street was a library. Behind them was Washington Square. They started walking.

"I've got a lot on my mind," he said. "I don't have much stamina and I don't want to get hurt."

"You don't want to get hurt," Julia said.

He squinted at her. "You came here to test me, didn't you?" They had stopped for a traffic signal.

"I did not come here to test you," she said. She watched the light release them from the curb.

"I don't blame you," Frank said, putting out his hand as if he were showing her around. "You have a steady life, a steady man. Why give that up for me?"

In Paris, Frank had watched her continually, as if the next thing she would do fascinated him. Now he hardly looked at her. She wanted to tell him about the comedian but the time wasn't right.

"I don't know this part of the Village," he said. "I don't have any idea where we can eat."

"It doesn't matter," Julia said. But it did. In Paris, he knew a lot of restaurants.

"I'm sick of eating in restaurants," he said.

They stopped in front of one with a neon skillet over the door. Breakfast specials were posted in the window.

"I don't have much money," Frank said.

"I have money," she said.

"I just want coffee," he said.

They went inside. A short man in a black suit came to their booth. He looked overdressed.

"Eat something," Julia said. "You look thin."

"You've forgotten how thin I was in Paris," Frank said.

Julia ordered a club sandwich. She didn't like club sandwiches. Frank ordered coffee and the man went away.

"I have to make a tape this afternoon and get it over to a club. If they like it maybe I'll get a job. If they don't I'll have to borrow money from my sister."

Julia didn't know he had a sister.

"I'm trying to survive, Julia," he said.

"So is everyone else," she said. "I'm sorry." She looked at her hands. "I came to New York to see you. What am I supposed to do?"

"Visit your friend like you told your husband you were going to."

"Paulette is getting an abortion."

"It sounds like she needs you."

The waiter set a club sandwich on the table. He poured Frank more coffee.

"I thought you loved me," Julia said in a low voice. She looked at Frank over the waiter's sleeve. The waiter seemed enormous standing there.

"I could love you but I'm not going to let myself," Frank said.

Julia stared at him. Then she looked up at the waiter.

"He has a lot of willpower, doesn't he?" she said.

The waiter put down the check. Julia picked it up and walked to the cashier. Beside the cash register was a vase with a rose in it.

Julia watched it blur and closed her fingers over the warm coins the woman put in her palm.

Julia felt light-headed. They were back on the street with nowhere to go. She watched an American flag hang limp against the sky behind Frank. He took hold of her shoulders and squeezed. He kissed her throat. He kissed her mouth. The softness of his lips made her want to stay. She bit his tongue.

Julia turned away and started walking. She looked back once. Frank was a stranger standing there watching her.

"I had an anesthetic this time," said Paulette. She was sitting on her sofa with a quilt over her lap. Julia poured them both some wine. "At least it was easier than the last time."

The chair in which Julia sat was upholstered in silk. Paulette's little boy was asleep in the next room and her husband Randall lived in a hotel.

"Charles speaks four languages. Spanish, French, German, and some African dialect. I believe he even knows a little Arabic. He writes marvelous letters," said Paulette.

Was he kind? Was he a good lover? Julia took a sip of wine. Paulette was pale but she looked elegant and Julia felt plain. Julia had always felt plain around Paulette, who even in college seemed in exquisite control.

"He's married," said Paulette. "Naturally that complicates things in some ways. But in other ways, I prefer it." Paulette put the rim of the wine glass to her mouth but did not drink. She stared at the baseboard across the room.

"Maybe you shouldn't drink wine on top of the anesthetic," said Julia.

"I won't drink much," said Paulette. "Now tell me about Frank."

"He's a musician I met in Paris. We were lovers for a week. I thought about leaving Michael."

"You have a right to go after what you want in life," said Paulette. "Look at me."

"But Frank isn't the way I remembered." Julia pulled her feet up onto the chair.

"They never are," said Paulette. "I had three affairs before Randall and I broke up."

"In Paris, Frank acted crazy about me," Julia said.

"Were you crazy about him?"

"Oh yes," Julia said. "In Paris we were crazy about each other."

Already the memory was growing untidy and dim. She wanted to make it disappear.

JULIA *and michael go to anna's wedding*

Julia sat at the kitchen table. Michael was still in bed. He had been sleeping late every morning. She raised her right foot and pushed out the heel to stretch the Achilles tendon. Since New York she hadn't had any energy.

"Don't you have anything besides instant?" Michael said. He stood in the doorway in his underwear.

"I ran out," said Julia. She gave him the cup of coffee she had fixed for herself. He stood there sipping it.

"What do you want?" she said.

"I want to wake up. I want real coffee."

"Are you hungry?" she said.

He turned and left without answering her. She heard him go back upstairs. She turned on "Good Morning, America" to drown out his presence in the house. Then she felt lonely.

"Wait a minute," she said when she heard the front door click open. She went out into the living room.

"What," said Michael.

"How much longer is this going to go on?" she said. She stepped forward and put her arms around him. He didn't move.

"I'm sick of looking for a job and not finding one," he said. "You know that."

"Why won't you let yourself need me?" she said. "Tell me what you want and I'll do it."

"I want real coffee. I want you to clean the house. I want you to start inviting our friends over for dinner." He walked out the door.

"Cabbage, thirty-seven cents. Instant mashed potatoes, ninety-nine," said the clerk.

He was the only one in the store who called out each item and price. Julia wondered what made him do this. He rang up the total for the old woman ahead of Julia in the checkout line. It was apparent she had no one to take care of her or she would not wear such a coat on a warm day. Loneliness made people cold, thought Julia. The woman squinted at the figures on the cash register. She paid with food stamps.

"And how are you today?" the clerk asked Julia as he bagged the old woman's groceries. He put a stalk of celery in last. The leaves stuck out of the top of the brown bag.

"I'm fine," said Julia.

His cheerfulness was nauseating. She looked at the magazines in the rack beside her. On the cover of *Good Housekeeping* was a blurb about keeping sex alive in marriage. Julia started putting her groceries on the counter. In her shopping cart were chocolate ripple ice cream, processed hot-pepper cheese, imitation-butter crackers with real sesame seeds, frozen waffles, Aunt Jemima's imitation-flavored maple syrup, a family pack of chicken legs, potatoes, canned spaghetti sauce, all things Michael liked that she never bought.

"Seventy-three twenty-three," said the cashier. He sang it out. As Julia wrote a check, he chatted to her about the soaring price of groceries.

Outside, Julia saw the old woman put her groceries into a taxi. Julia pushed her cart across the street toward her car. When she looked back, the groceries and the woman were inside the cab and the driver was pulling away.

"You don't expect me to go, do you?" Julia said.

"Yes," said Michael.

"Why should I?" she said.

She put slices of pepper cheese on a wooden plate. Michael pulled a tray of ice cubes out of the freezer.

"David's firm might make me an offer," he said.

"Oh great," she said. "So you're going to be working with the new husband of your ex-wife. And we'll get to see them often. That's swell." She knew she was being unreasonable. She ripped open the sesame-seed crackers.

"Stop being childish," he said. He twisted the plastic ice tray. Cubes popped out and slid across the kitchen floor. "Nobody's trying to take anything away from you," he said.

"What do I have that you could take away?" She laughed.

Michael bent down to pick up the ice cubes.

"If I had been married to some flashy guy and wanted you to be bosom buddies, you'd refuse," Julia said.

"If you got to know Anna, you'd like her. She's a nice person." Michael held out a handful of ice cubes.

Julia took them and threw them into the sink. "Not a chance," she said.

Michael stared at her. "What's wrong with you?" he shouted. "What goes through your mind?"

"Why don't you go alone?" Julia said.

"It would look funny," he said.

"I knew it," she said. "I knew you were worried about what people will think." Her arms were tingling. Her chest had probably broken out.

"Try to act like a grown-up, Julia," Michael said.

"Oh Christ," said Julia.

"What's wrong?"

She started crying.

"Just do it," he said.

"All right," she said.

Anna's hand was warm and moist. Julia saw the braveness in her smile.

"I've heard so much about you," said Julia.

"You have?" said Anna.

"All good things," said Julia. If Anna didn't stop bleaching her hair it would break off. But her complexion was light and flawless. Julia looked down the reception line to her right. Two women in pastel floor-length gowns seemed to be trying to make eye contact with everyone.

"I hope you have a happy life," said Julia. But Anna was already looking past her. Julia thought she was looking for Michael. Then Michael stepped forward. Julia wondered if he felt any regret. She heard him wish Anna good luck.

Julia stepped out of the line and went to the bar. She ordered a double Scotch on the rocks. Everyone was only pretending to have a good time, she thought as she looked around the room. At least one person ought to be honest. She took her drink over to the hors d'oeuvres table. She ate some salmon mousse.

"There you are," said Alice. She hugged Julia almost without touching her. "We haven't seen you in ages. Where have you been?"

"I've been to Cairo and Paris," said Julia.

"I heard," said Alice. She clasped her hands between her breasts. "I'm dying to hear all about it. How is Michael? Has he found a job yet?"

"Not yet," said Julia.

"You know Bob is looking, too," said Alice. "I know how it is."
Julia rolled her eyes and nodded.

"Sometimes, honestly, I don't think I can stand it another minute," said Alice.

"Does he take it out on you?" said Julia.

"I can't do anything right. The last time this happened, about three years ago, I tried to be sweet and understanding. Do you know what he did?"

"What?" said Julia.

"He said I was crazy. I said okay, then let's go to a psychiatrist. We'll see who's crazy. He said okay. He thought, you know, the psychiatrist would tell me what my problem was."

"I can guess what happened," said Julia.

"I told this doctor how things were and you-know-who turned out to have the problem."

Julia glanced at a woman behind Alice, then pulled her eyes back.

"So if you want to get some perspective, go to a psychiatrist. Talk fast. Keep it light. I'm sure he'll tell you you're fine."

Julia thought about telling Alice that she had been to a psychiatrist, but she didn't feel that close to Alice. Why was Alice telling her all this?

"I'm telling you this so you'll know you're not alone," said Alice. "We all go through it. You finally realize you might as well keep the one you've got because they're all the same."

"That's a little discouraging," said Julia.

"Bob went through a phase when he came home and cried every night," Alice said. "I thought he was going crazy. Finally he snapped out of it. I never did know what was wrong."

"Did you ask him?" Julia was touched by the thought of Bob crying.

"No," said Alice. "He didn't want my help so I ignored him."

131

"Oh dear," said Julia.

"Hang in there," Alice said. She looked as if nothing ever bothered her.

Julia watched Alice walk across the room. Maybe her marriage to Michael wasn't as bad as she thought. If she were married to someone else, things would be different but they probably wouldn't be any better. Marriage isn't what you think it is, she thought. The words were in her mouth. She almost shouted them.

JULIA *and michael go sailing*

"I'm going sailing," Michael said at dinner.

"With whom?" said Julia.

"This friend of mine, Chuck Robinson. You don't know him. We're talking about hanging out a shingle together."

"Who else is going?"

"His girlfriend and a friend of hers."

"Another woman."

"That's right."

"You mean two men and two women."

"That's correct."

"Am I invited?"

"I don't think there's room," said Michael. "Look. I don't even know the other woman. It's just four people going sailing." He glared at her. "Pass the potatoes."

She passed the potatoes.

"Michael. What is going on."

"I want some time to myself," he said.

"But you won't be by yourself. You'll be in very close quarters with a strange woman."

"I want to spend some time away from you," said Michael.

"That hurts," said Julia. What he proposed seemed unfair. For weeks she'd felt no curiosity about other men. Julia was embarrassed, looking back at Jim and Frank. She no longer felt like that impetuous woman.

"I didn't think you would be interested," Michael said.

"Look at this dinner. I hate meat loaf. I made it for you," she said.

"Julia. It's cold out there this time of year."

"I won't complain."

"I really need to spend some time with Chuck."

"Have lunch with him. Invite him over to dinner. Michael, let's charter our own boat. Let's take a trip, just the two of us. We need time together. Let's try to work things out." She couldn't stand the thought of him with another woman.

In the night the sky cracked with light and sound. The storm went on and on. Sometimes they could see the harbor across the bay and the masts of the sailboats tied up there. The rain drummed on the cabin and the boat swung on the anchor line. Julia got up every hour to check the anchor. Michael was on deck the last time she went topside. They said nothing to each other. She gave him her foul-weather jacket. Back in their berth she listened to the rigging beat in the wind. It sounded like a pagan ritual. If they lived through it, everything would be all right. She awoke at dawn when one of the halyards began to clang against the mast. Michael got up to tie it off.

"There's a man setting out crab pots off the dock," she said to Michael below.

Julia was drinking coffee in the cockpit. They were in a small cove near a white farmhouse with a private dock. The cove was lined with trees, mostly oak. The rinsed air felt cool on her skin.

She studied the white-haired man kneeling at the end of the dock. He looked as if he belonged there. He looked kind.

"Do you want to go into the village this morning?" Michael called up.

"Not really," she said. "The wind's good. Let's sail."

"I need to get to a phone and I want a newspaper," he said.

Julia told herself it did not matter what they did. Still, she was irritated. They were supposed to be on vacation. She watched the man pick up a bucket, step into the powerboat tied to the dock, and start to bail. He shook his head and smiled at something. Julia tossed her coffee overboard. Getting out of his boat, the man glanced at her. If he looked again, she decided, she would wave. But he didn't. He walked up the dock with his hand on his chest as if he had pain there. Below, Michael was cursing and slamming drawers shut. Michael would never change, she thought.

As the man's white head ducked into the cab of his pickup, Julia spotted a blue heron flapping across the sky. She saw the man watch it, too, his arms over the steering wheel as he leaned forward to look through the upper part of the windshield. Julia wanted a man who would stop to watch a heron. The heron flew to the other side of the cove and landed in the water where it stood still, a thin, blue ghost against the dark trees. She heard the truck start up as she climbed out of the cockpit, stubbing her toe on the sheet block. The pain made her so angry, she felt nauseated. She looked into the water and dug her nails into her forearm. The sun reflected brightly off the stanchions now.

"Let's get going," Michael said, his head appearing in the gang-way. He was getting a dark tan.

Michael started the engine and told her to pull up anchor. From the bow she looked at the white house. The truck was parked in front of it but the man was not in sight. Michael started moving the boat up on the anchor and Julia pulled in the line, letting it fall into the locker under the deck at her feet. When the bow was directly over the anchor, she cleated off the line and let the boat pull the anchor free. She turned to signal Michael. He was looking at the house. The boat swung around and moved toward the dock.

"Michael," she shouted. "Watch where we're going."

He looked at the chart beside him. She shouted again and pointed toward the dock. Still, Michael studied the chart. The powerboat and the dock were coming up on the starboard side as if they, not she and Michael, were moving. Julia screamed at Michael but the morning seemed to absorb her voice. She threw herself on the port deck beside the cabin and hid her eyes in her arms. After a few minutes she looked up. The dock was behind them and they were headed out of the cove.

"What got into you?" Michael shouted.

"I thought we were going to hit that man's dock," she shouted back, standing. Michael smiled a cocky half-smile and steered the boat out into the channel, advancing the throttle.

Julia believed what she had seen, yet there had been no crash. She looked at the choppy water. The sun reflected off the waves like pieces of shattered glass. She could tell she wasn't going to leave him.

"I'm not sure we ought to stay married," Michael said.

Julia put her hand over her heart and stopped breathing. Michael lit a cigarette. They had just finished eating.

"Why do you say that?" she said.

"I've been feeling pretty indifferent toward you," he said.

Indifference was worse than dislike. The danger was real.

"I'm not enthusiastic about this marriage," he said.

"I never thought you were enthusiastic," she said.

Michael's face was still. "Look babe. We don't have much in common anymore," he said.

"We have similar backgrounds," she said. "We both like to sail." She listened to herself defending their marriage.

"Tell me the truth," Michael said. "Are you happy?"

"The problem is," said Julia, "that you don't want to be close." She got up to clear the dishes.

"Do you really believe you're easy to be close to?" he said. "I don't even think I'm important to you."

"What is important to me?" she said.

"Music? I don't know what else you think about." Michael reached up and turned out a light. "I hope we're not pulling too much off that battery," he said.

Julia slammed the plates down into the sink. They were plastic and didn't break. "Why do you always do that?" she said.

"Would you rather have a dead battery in the morning?" he shouted.

"Don't be ridiculous," she said. She squirted soap into the sink and turned on the tap.

Michael stubbed out his cigarette in the ashtray. He got up and opened the hatch. Julia was standing at the sink with her hands in the soapy water. She stared at Michael's cigarette still burning in the ashtray.

"Put that out," she said. "You're giving me cancer."

Michael crushed the cigarette.

"Remember the night you shoved my head in the dog's dish and tried to strangle me?" she said.

"I didn't try to strangle you," Michael said.

"I like to think you did," said Julia. "I like to think it was passion." She stared at him. "The only time I feel good with you is when we're fighting."

"That's nuts," he said. "I don't feel good when we're fighting." He sat down, then stood up again. "Sometimes I wish you would find someone else."

"So you could divorce me?" she said. She'd never thought he cared enough about marriage to want a divorce.

"Why did you marry me in the first place?" Michael asked.

Julia let the water out of the sink. The bilge pump switched on. She listened to it moan.

"When I was a kid," she said, "we went on these horrible car trips. I used to hold a sign up to the window that said HELP! I'M BEING KIDNAPPED. I wished I were being kidnapped. I wanted somebody to take me away on an adventure."

Michael looked at her quickly, then away. "What's that supposed to mean?" he said.

"When we got married, I thought you were going to take me on an adventure," she said.

JULIA *finds a divorce lawyer*

"Is there another man?" he asked.

Julia said no. This seemed truthful. She wouldn't leave Michael for anyone she knew.

Rodney Steigerman tipped his chair back on two legs. He lit a cigar. Julia had picked his name out of the yellow pages because the sound of it gave her confidence. Rodney was short, round, and bald. His lips were set in a pout.

"We have to put down a reason," Rodney said. He held up a divorce agreement as if he held a mouse by its tail.

"Can we say due to lack of interest?" she asked.

"Won't he sleep with you?" Rodney put down the piece of paper.

"That isn't it." Julia looked at her hands.

"Does he abuse you?"

"He almost hit me once," she said.

"Does he abuse you emotionally?"

"He isn't enthusiastic about what I do." She glanced out the window behind Rodney at the dirty sunlight between buildings.

"What do you do?" Rodney asked.

"I'm a musician."

"I see." He nodded and relit his cigar. "You want to have a career and he doesn't want you to."

"Not exactly." Julia looked at the piles of paper on Rodney's desk. He didn't have a secretary, or diplomas on his wall. She thought he had back trouble from the way he walked. "I want to play in nightclubs," she said.

"You want to play in nightclubs and he won't let you."

"He has never said I couldn't."

"Does he fool around?"

"Not to my knowledge."

"Maybe you could redescribe the problem for me," said Rodney.

"Very little happens. Days go by. He won't talk to me."

Rodney leaned forward with his elbows on the desk. "How long has he been giving you the silent treatment?" he asked.

"I meant we rarely have discussions. He doesn't like to talk about what happens to him. He's very private." Julia sighed.

"We're going to have to pin down the problem," Rodney said.

"I do believe he cares about me. I care about him." Julia spread her hands.

"You do?"

"I miss him when he's gone. But after he comes home, I feel more lonely than when he was away."

"Is he missing often?"

"What I mean is, he goes on business trips. While he's away I imagine things are going to be different," Julia said.

"How so?"

"I pretend he'll walk into the house and yell, 'Hey Julia, I'm home. I want to talk to you.' And then we have a conversation."

"What does he do when he gets home?"

"He turns on the news."

"What do you do?"

"I fix dinner."

"I knew a couple like this once." Rodney held his chin in his hands and puffed on the cigar. "They were very unhappy."

"What did they do?" Julia said. She watched Rodney's pudgy hands.

"They moved to L.A."

"I want to live with someone who talks to me," said Julia.

"Language is our problem," Rodney said. "I can get you a divorce if that's what you want. But we have to get the reason into some kind of language."

Madame Marie's place of business was downtown. The entrance was sandwiched between a health food store on the left and an Oriental carpet shop on the right. Julia opened the door and started up the narrow staircase leaving the bright day and traffic behind her. Madame Marie herself opened the door at the head of the stairs. She was fat. She wore a purple leotard with a red skirt over it. Her bracelets jangled.

"Come in, dear," she said, her voice rich and unfriendly.

The velour furniture reminded Julia of the airport bar in Athens.

"Sit down in that chair," said Madame Marie. She disappeared through a doorway with a curtain over it. When she reappeared, nothing had changed. She sat in the chair across from Julia.

"Tell me your first name, age, and birthdate, sweetheart," she said.

Julia told her. Madame Marie took Julia's right hand but did not look at it. She looked over Julia's shoulder and squinted her eyes. Julia was afraid of her.

"I see a man in the future," she said. She made circles with her index finger on Julia's palm. "I do not know who he is. Wait a minute." She closed her eyes. She began to hum. She made more circles. "He is a musician. You already know this man. He will be a disappointment. Are you a musician?" Madame Marie asked, opening her eyes.

"Yes," said Julia.

Madame Marie closed her eyes again. She shook her head.

"What is it?" said Julia.

"You will live a long life," she said as if this were of little consequence. "You will struggle a long time before getting what you want."

"How long will it be before I am successful?" Julia said. She thought she had struggled long enough already.

"That isn't what I'm talking about. I talk about the heart."

"Will I stay with my husband?" she said.

"That is another question. I see some times of happiness, some times of sorrow."

"What are you talking about then?" Julia said.

"You are looking all around you for answers that only lie within."

Julia wanted more for her money. "Will I have children?" she said.

"I see the possibility of one child," Madame Marie said looking directly into Julia's eyes. "You see how you look all around you?"

"What am I supposed to be looking for?" Julia asked with impatience. Michael was the one who left the big hole in her.

"You will know when you find it."

Julia sighed.

"I have many friends who can pray for you. They will make a spiritual tent to ensure that your dreams come true. To light a candle is only twenty dollars."

"I don't see how that can help if I'm supposed to find my own way," said Julia.

Madame Marie smiled sadly and shook her head.

"All right," said Julia.

"Tomorrow evening at eight o'clock sit quietly for one hour."

"Tomorrow evening I will be at a dinner party," said Julia.

"We can postpone it," said Madame Marie.

"I don't think so," said Julia. She stood up. On the wall behind Madame Marie was a picture of Christ.

"Find the door to your own heart," Madame Marie said in an impersonal voice. It sounded like common advice.

Julia looked at Madame Marie for more, but she could tell her time was up.

JULIA *and michael*
have a conversation

"I called to say I love you," a man's voice said over the phone.

"I'm sorry?" Julia said.

"What's wrong, lover? Can't you talk?"

"I can talk."

"Look, I haven't got much time. I just wanted to call."

Julia recognized the voice. It belonged to the man she had been waiting for. It was deep and convincing. She would do anything this voice asked her to do.

"I won't be able to talk to you for a few days. Jolene?"

"Yes," Julia said.

"I won't be able to call you, lover. But I'll be thinking about you." The sound of a kiss came over the phone. The line went dead.

"Good-bye," Julia said to the receiver. She felt the kiss in her ear.

She had found him in pieces. His hair, hands, shoulders, eyes, and voice belonged to different men. Julia looked at the pieces of men in her mind. She looked at the pieces of herself. When Michael got home she was still sitting in the wing chair contemplating the pieces.

"Are you okay?" he asked.

"I don't know," she said.

Michael stood in front of her. "What's wrong?" he said.

"Nothing changes. I wish something would change," she said.

"Isn't that up to you, babe?"

Julia did not want to hear this.

"What do you want to happen?" Michael asked.

"I want to get a gig. I want to have fun. I want you to talk to me."

Michael removed his topcoat. He tossed it onto the sofa. "I'm talking to you," he said.

"I want to hear you say you love me," said Julia. She watched him pace.

He jingled some coins in his pocket. "I've been under a lot of pressure," he said.

"Is that what it was?" she said without interest.

"Why don't we go out for dinner?" he said. "Let's go over to McGraw's. I want to talk to you." He picked up his coat again.

"At a boy," a man shouted as they walked into McGraw's. Crowd sounds came from the television above the bar.

"Pitcher of beer?" Irene called to them.

Michael said yes and waved to the bartender. Irene brought the pitcher to their booth.

"What'll it be?" she asked.

"Crab cakes," said Julia.

"I'll have the chowder and crab cakes," Michael said.

"Why does everybody want crab cakes tonight?" Irene asked. She walked away.

"She's talkative," Julia said.

"I hear she has a new boyfriend," he said.

Julia looked at Irene. She had put her hair up and she was wearing a fancy white blouse. "I'd like to feel that way myself," Julia said.

"The grass looks greener, but it isn't," Michael said as if she already knew the story.

"What do you mean by that?" Julia asked. She hoped he was going to tell her he had done something terrible.

"I have a confession," he said. "Betsy Flower asked me over to her place for a drink last week. To celebrate my new job."

"Betsy doesn't have anything to do with your new job," Julia said quickly.

"I was ready to leave and we were standing by the door," Michael said. "I kissed her. I could have slept with her but I didn't."

"Self-restraint does come in handy," Julia said.

"Damn it, Julia. I'm trying to tell you something," Michael said.

Julia was angry. "Then say it," she said.

"I love you."

"You do?"

"You might think you've found someone better but you don't really know them. Betsy would drive me crazy," he said. He poured more beer.

"Here you go, folks," Irene said. She set their plates on the table. "Can I get you anything else?" She walked away.

"I went to see a divorce lawyer," Julia said.

"You did?" Michael looked at her. "What did he say?"

"He couldn't pin down the problem."

Michael laughed. "Where did you find this guy?" he asked.

"There's something strange going on between us, Michael," she said.

Michael picked up his spoon.

"I don't even know how you feel most of the time," Julia said.

He blew on his soup. "I just told you I love you. How much more do you want? Christ, this is hot." He put down the spoon.

"I don't know," Julia said.

For a moment Michael looked helpless, then pandemonium broke out in the room. His eyes found the television above the bar. "Son of a bitch," he said.

Julia stared at Michael's cuff link. Maybe she was looking for a man who didn't exist. He might only be an idea of hers. Then she thought she saw him again, sitting alone at a table against the wall. He was writing on a napkin.

"I'm sorry babe," Michael said, "but I'd like to see the end of this game. I'll be right back."

Julia sat there. The game was almost over, she told herself, and then they would finish their conversation. The man against the wall stopped writing and took a sip of beer. For a moment the room was still, then the people at the bar exploded into whistling and shouting. Julia took a bite of cold crab cake. The people at the bar started booing. She glanced up at the television. The game had gone into overtime.

Julia slipped out of the wooden booth with her coat and walked to the bar. She tapped Michael on the shoulder. "I hate basketball," she said. "I'm going home."

"Okay babe," he said in a friendly voice.

"Fine," she said and walked away.

Outside, the night air was frosty. Julia turned and looked through McGraw's window. She saw Michael, his faced raised and luminous in the light from the television. He was yelling without sound, his mouth wide open. A city bus roared to a stop at the curb behind her. She got on.

Inside, the bus was warm and well lit. Julia sat next to the window. She sat and watched herself ride through the city.